The Blood of Destiny

A NOVEL

by

SEAN LEARY

Very special thanks, as always, to my son, Jackson. Everything I do, I dedicate to you, my best friend and beautiful boy. I love you.

Very special thanks as well to Matthew and Pam Clemens, for your incredible support, advice and friendship. I'll never forget it.

Thanks as well to Nichole Senger, Linda Cook, Bill and Gail Leary, Dan O'Shea and Johanna Harris and all of my friends, fans and readers everywhere, particularly my readers and friends on Facebook.

ISBN # (Print book) 978-0615990453

Library of Congress Catalog Card Number: Applied for

First edition print: 4/12/2014

Cover design and interior design by Sean Leary.

Website: www.seanleary.com. Email: seanleary@seanleary.com.

As always,

For Jackson

What Critics Are Saying About 'The Arimathean' Trilogy and 'The Blood of Destiny'...

"This book rocks. That pretty much says it all. It just rocks. It really is a non-stop, action-packed popcorn book where the fun never ends. I enjoyed reading it immensely. I'm really looking forward to the sequels."

--- Matthew Clemens
Best-selling author, "No One Will Hear You."

"A real surprise, in a great way... a non-stop thrill ride of action! Full of huge thrills and stunning twists, smart writing and surprising heart. A book that will please action fans and fans of Christian fantasy alike, while pandering to neither. And in the end, a book of endless entertainment that makes you think, about life, about faith and about what drives us... a must-read."

--- Alison Baker
Yahoo! News Chicago

"Wow! Sean Leary is the new Stephen King."
--- Geeta Razack
The Geeta Razack Blog

"At first, when Sean Leary described his new novel `The Arimathean,' I thought he had lost it. Ninjas and the Nativity – seriously? But he tells it here with seriousness and, above all, respect, with dialogue that fleshes out his characters and solid action that keeps the reader turning the pages. And don't skip to the last pages or you'll cheat yourself out of a finale that's truly grand."

--- Linda Cook
Award-winning critic / Iowa Press Women

"It takes a lively and inventive writer to cast the three wise men as ninja wizards. It takes a great writer to enrich and deepen such a high concept notion and create an exciting and compelling story as Sean Leary has done with 'The Arimathean.'"

--- Sean Patrick
Morning show host, WOC-AM

"Imaginative and moving at the same time."

--- Father John Comerford
Joliet Catholic Academy

"Lovely imagery… very nice descriptive turns of phrase."

--- Connie Corcoran Wilson
Best-selling author, "Hellfire and Damnnation"

"A bloody, gory, fight-filled adventure story… but here's the thing: this book is UPLIFTING. Gross at times, yes, intense throughout, definitely. But it also has that feel good quality a good adventure story must have. Whether you take that as a "Glory of God" message or just a "it feels awesome to kick evil's ass" message is up to you. The book puts no pressure on you to choose. Just enjoy the ride whatever way you want."

--- William Pepper
The William Pepper Blog

"I highly recommend anyone to read, "The Arimethean" and "Blood Of Destiny". Sean has a beautiful way of making the Bible come to life. All in this series read as smoothly as viewing a movie. Beautifully depicted."

--- Jennifer Sergeant
Author, Courage To Rise Above

"An incredibly cool concept – ninja wizards for the win! – and an even more awesome book. It's not just an amazing idea that Sean Leary's got here, it's a rockin' adventure story with a ton of action, but a surprising amount of heart. It'll thrill you with its imagination and cliffhangers, throw you a ton of curves and leave you wondering what's going to happen next and then out of the blue make you really think about these people and feel for what they're going through. A masterfully written book."

--- *Alternate Waves Comix Zine*

"There aren't a lot of writers who would have the courage to rewrite the stories of the Bible, let alone rewrite them with ninjas, but Sean Leary does it with surprising fun, imagination and sensitivity to the subject matter. Leary doesn't just parody the Bible or make fun of the stories, he gives them the proper respect and reverence, just looking at things from another angle – one which is fantastic and entertaining. Leary understands that the lines between religious text, fantasy writing and mythology are thin and he manages to deftly handle skating along them, satisfying fans of each. It's masterful writing, with great action-adventure sequences and heartfelt and sincere tales of redemption in line with the source material."

--- *Ian Fox*
The Foxforce Files Blog

INTRODUCTION

When I mapped out the Arimathean trilogy, there was a pretty logical stopping point for each book, based upon story ideas I had carried with me since I was a child, raised on Catholic school and J.R.R. Tolkien.

The first book, The Arimathean, revolves around Christ's birth, incorporating my idea of the Magi as ninja wizards.

The third book revolves around the second coming, the book of Revelation and the idea of the immortal guardian – one man who is stationed (or condemned, depending on your perspective) to walk the earth until Christ arrives again.

The second book? Well, obviously it had to involve Christ's death and resurrection.

Which led me to the disciples and Mary Magdalene as the heroes, fighting Satan to safeguard Christ's body, during the three days between his death and resurrection, to prevent it from being turned into the antichrist.

For a long time, I've been fascinated by the characters around Jesus. Especially Magdalene. In doing research, I found that the common perception of her as a prostitute is erroneous and that it could be due to a variety of misinterpretations or biases. I've always liked strong female characters, especially in action genres (e.g. Buffy the Vampire Slayer) so the thought of making Magdalene not only a powerful warrior, but the most powerful of the disciples was very appealing. That's why she shows up in book one of the trilogy, along with Simon Peter, Jude and Judas – the others' whose power rivals her own. By establishing them as warriors from youth, it sets the stage for their later power.

I also chose Simon Peter because he is depicted in the Bible as being a warrior – he is the apostle who cuts off the centurion's ear when Christ is attacked in Gethsemane. Although that side of him is definitely downplayed, you get the feeling he's not just some pacifist fisherman or farmer.

At first, I was going to have those four be the power base during the battles – Magdalene, Simon Peter and Jude joining the Magi and Arimathean against Judas and his demon armies. But it was much more interesting to have the disciples be more than hippies in distress, so to speak. It was far cooler and offered more potential for excitement to paint them as a cadre of elite warriors.

To me, in this book, the apostles are like the Seven Samurai (or, if you prefer, the Magnificent Seven) – a deadly array of heroes hand-picked by the secret society of the Silent Hand to protect the Christ.

And once I came up with that idea, the fun really started.

And it is fun. It has been fun, to write this book and the first in the trilogy, to map out the third, and it will likely be fun to write book three as well. I hope you, the reader, feel that palpable sense of enjoyment, action and adventure.

As I've said before, I mean no offense with this trilogy. I was raised Catholic and through the years I've investigated a number of different religions but I've always remained a believer.

With these books, I'm expressing those beliefs in an unorthodox and imaginative way, but their integrity is there and you'll find it in the respectful manner in which I treat the characters. The traditionally good characters are good and the traditionally evil characters are evil. But within those broad outlines I've tried to humanize them, to make them more accessible and understandable to modern audiences. I feel that gives them greater resonance and impact, both within the confines of these stories and outside them as well.

There are two questions that have come up often during my book signings for the first book of this trilogy.

First question: Am I trying to convert people? No. People are going to follow the path they want to follow. I certainly don't have the power to change them. I'm just a storyteller. I'm writing entertaining tales with an ultimately positive message. As with all of my stories, people can read them for solely entertainment, or if they're so inclined, they can look deeper. There are a lot of layers to the work, but the surface is pretty fun all by itself.

The other question, or variations of it: Who am I to rewrite the Bible with ninjas? Don't I think that's blasphemous?

No, I don't feel it's blasphemous. As I tell people, I'm just a writer. I was inspired to do this, and if you believe in God, you believe that positive inspiration comes from Him. I don't know why these ideas blossomed in my imagination all those years ago or why, now, decades later, the stories have finally arrived in my mind, ready to be written. But I can't see that it's a bad thing in any way. I think if you actually read the stories and see what I'm doing, you'll see that I am handling the characters and the material in a respectful manner. You'll see that I'm writing stories that will entertain and appeal to believers and non-believers alike. And, just maybe, as you read them, you'll find yourself enjoying them.

That's my most fervent hope. That people read them and enjoy them. And if that's all you get from the experience, a good time, that's cool with me. But, like I said, if you want more, it's there, if you want to find it.

Either way, enjoy the trip.

Sean Leary

APPENDICES

For utilization and clarification:

Timeline of the action in The Blood of Destiny

Character Index

Prelude (what has come before)

TIMELINE (approximate)

Chapter one	4 p.m. Friday
Chapter two	4 p.m. Friday
Chapter three	4-5 p.m. Friday
Chapter four	5 p.m. Friday
Chapter five	5 p.m. Friday
Chapter six	5-6 p.m. Friday
Chapter seven	5-6 p.m. Friday
Chapter eight	5-6 p.m. Friday
Chapter nine	6 p.m. Friday
Chapter ten	flashback
Chapter eleven	6-7 p.m. Friday
Chapter twelve	7 p.m. Friday
Chapter thirteen	7 p.m. Friday
Chapter fourteen	7 p.m. Friday
Chapter fifteen	flashback
Chapter sixteen	8 p.m. Friday
Chapter seventeen	8 p.m. Friday
Chapter eighteen	8 p.m. Friday
Chapter nineteen	9 p.m. Friday
Chapter twenty	10-12 p.m. Friday
Chapter twenty-one	10-12 p.m. Friday
Chapter twenty-two	10-12 p.m. Friday
Chapter twenty-three	4 a.m. Saturday

INDEX OF NAMES AND CHARACTERS

The Arimathean...... warrior, former and future Magi

Balthazar...............Magi

Gaspar..................Magi

Melchior...............Magi

Jesus Christ....... Messiah

Mary....... Mother of Jesus

Joseph...... father of Jesus (deceased)

John the Revelator....disciple, One Who Walks Between Worlds, associate of the Magi and the Arimathean

Magdalene........disciple, apprentice to the Revelator

James....... disciple, One Who Walks Between Worlds

Matthias.................apprentice to the Revelator

Tanara......apprentice to Magdalene and the Arimathean

Simon Peter..........disciple, one of the Sons of Thunder

Jude................disciple, one of the Sons of Thunder

Bartholomew.......disciple, Scorpion of 1000 Stings

Matthew..........disciple, The Shadow Blade

Thomas........disciple, The All-Seeing Eye

Philip.........disciple, the One who Cheated Death

Andrew.....disciple, the One who Cheated Death

Simon the Zealot......disciple

James Alphaeus..... disciple, the Cobra's Strike

Judas Iscariot.... Former disciple, betrayer of Christ

Kudi...... a journey through death into the netherworlds

Magi.... noble order of magickal warriors

Saturnari.....evil order or magickal warriors

Kailani X'ett..... patron warrior priestess of the Magi

S'iam B'ala..... the Golden City, where the Magi dwell, a city which dwells between dimensions and worlds

Soulsfire..... holy sword of the Arimathean

Heavensblade..... holy sword of Balthazar

Arantioch...... golden soulsblade of Tanara

Seraphim..... Balthazar's familiar

Cherubim.....Melchior's familiar

Electrum......Gaspar's familiar

Satan...... ultimate evil, ruler of hell

Gundari..... wolven demons of the old caste of hell

Oostynynthyne....ancient demon collective

R'aall'akai..... demon of the ancient planes

Nostrenemi...... flea-like demons of the ancient planes

Syylavius..... demon collective from the nether regions

Lucisfang...... Judas Iscariot's ebonblade

Herod Antipas..... Judean king

Pontius Pilate..... Roman governor of Judea

Tiberius....... Roman Emperor

Lknng'tthr..... Herod Antipas' vizier

Herod... Antipas' father, former Judean king (deceased)

PRELUDE

What has come before:

In 1 AD, the three Magi were summoned from the Glowing City of S'iam B'ala, the city between worlds, by the mysterious earth-bound secret society The Silent Hand. The three most powerful ninja wizards of the twin dimensions – Balthazar, Melchior and Gaspar – accepted a mission to protect a young couple, Joseph and Mary, about to give birth to a child seers predicted would be the prophesized Messiah.

In order to facilitate their trek to the holy city of Bethlehem for the birth, the Magi enlisted a former member of their order, the most fearsome swordsman on earth, the Arimathean. In exchange for the Magi's help in seeking revenge against the slayer of his wife and children, the Arimathean agreed to accompany them.

Along the way, the then-king of Judea, Herod, conspiring with the Roman governor Pontius Pilate, and the ruler of the underworld, Satan, unleashed a torrent of demons upon the travelers, hellspawn led by the half-human, half-demon son of King Herod, the diabolical Herodius, the murderer of the Arimathean's family.

After lengthy battles with an array of demonic forces, and strategic unions with a variety of accomplices (including John the Revelator, Mary Magdalene and future disciples Simon Peter and Jude, among others), the Magi and Arimathean were able to get the couple to Bethlehem safely and the Arimathean killed Herodius, gaining his revenge.

The child of Joseph and Mary, named Jesus, called the Christ, was born.

After the birth, the Magi took the child and his parents into exile in Alexandria, Egypt. Various prophecies stated that two years after the child's birth, Herod would have an open window to slay the infant and the king, notorious for his bloodshed, would no doubt utilize that chance to destroy the Christ. However, with the Christ removed and in Egypt, he was spared.

During the ensuing thirty years, the Christ and his family, under protection of the Magi and Arimathean, would return to their home land with intermittent travels during the adolescence and young adulthood of the Christ. Jesus would finally settle in his home land, in 30 AD, to begin his ministry and start preaching and gathering followers.

The Silent Hand, knowing well the Christ was also prophesized to be in constant danger, and was destined to die in 33 AD, clandestinely assigned a number of their finest warriors to act as Jesus' closest friends and disciples.

These men – Simon Peter, Jude, Bartholomew, Matthew, Thomas, Philip, Andrew, Simon the Zealot, James Alphaeus, John the Revelator and his brother, James – were led by the woman warrior Mary Magdalene, and likewise joined by the man destined to betray Christ, Judas Iscariot.

On the night before Christ's death, Iscariot handed him over to an immense Roman force within the garden of Gethsemane. Christ was taken into custody, beaten, and dragged before the populace, who were asked to vote on which prisoner would be freed in accordance with Passover tradition – Jesus, or another man, convicted of inciting rebellion and stealing, Barabbas. The crowd chose Barabbas, and on a Friday afternoon, Christ was executed, murdered in satanic ritual upon the killing hill of Golgotha.

What the king, Herod Antipas, and his governor, Pilate – the men who ordered Christ slain – did not fully realize was that the Christ's death had been preordained, and that it was according to a plan to allow Jesus' soul to descend to hell and free the lost souls of purgatory, to allow them passage to heaven.

While the Christ died, the disciples remained in hiding, awaiting orders on what to do next. The prophecies declared that the Christ would rise on the morning of the third day after his death – the Sunday following his execution that Friday afternoon. The disciples would be tasked with protecting the Christ's body while they waited for his resurrection. However, until such a time as they were needed, they were asked to remain in a secret location often used as a hideaway by the Silent Hand.

Only Magdalene and her protégé, Tanara the Sin Eater, were allowed to stand in protection with Mary the mother of Jesus as she watched her son be crucified.

As *The Blood of Destiny* opens, Jesus has just died, and the Roman centurions who killed him and the two other prisoners sentenced to die on that day are peeling the bodies off the crosses, for use in other devious schemes…

THE BLOOD

OF

DESTINY

ONE

Thunder shook the firmament as the rain gently wept from the gray, washing the blood of the newly dead into the earth.

There were three.

Two beaten and lashed to the wood to choke in their own sweat and exhaustion.

And the third.

Tortured and tormented, haloed in thorns, cursed in unholy ritual and nailed, steel tearing his flesh, sealing it to the cross, to his doom, to his destiny.

All three, dead.

Their bodies limp and expired.

All being pulled from the implements of their doom, by the Roman centurions who had murdered them, bruising their final moments in scorn and ridicule, and even now refusing them dignity in death.

Grumbling as they yanked the limp corpses from their bloody crosses, the centurions tossed the bodies to the muddy ground, the rain washing their blood and gore into the earth.

The cries of mourners stained the air, but even as those who once loved and bore the condemned plead for their final peace, the soldiers denied it.

For beyond the shadows, creeping towards the freshly dead, just past Golgotha, the killing hill, were those whose gold warmed the palms of the Romans.

The Sodomites.

Sheathed in cloaks of crimson and wearing strange, unholy masks of sinister smirks and ornate jewels, delicate youthful curves covering their cruel animalistic urges.

They crept towards the muddy, blood soaked place slowly, slimily, emanating sick cooings beneath their facades as they appraised their new delights.

However, their path was cut short.

They stopped, slowly peered about nervously, as they felt a presence approaching.

Lightning slashed the sky like a fresh wound, the rain whipping the earth as the ebon figure scythed boldly through the tumult, towards the fields of the dead and damned.

And as the darkling approached from the shadows beyond them, striding purposely towards the grounds of slaughter, the Sodomites skittered and scattered to the edges of the hill of crucifixion, once more leaving the sorrowful to bid their farewells in peace as the soldiers dispensed with the duties of removing the dead.

Two men, one convicted of murder, one convicted of thievery.

And then, a third.

One crucified in the most violent and obscene manner.

Killed in ritual, according to the wishes of Herod Antipas, the king of their region.

He was the last to die.

And the only one mourned by anyone present.

A man named Jesus.

His mother, Mary, wept over the broken, beaten, lifeless body of her son, his blood mingling with the tears streaking down her cheeks as she held him close.

"Jesus," she wept softly. "My baby."

Clad in the ebon and violet ceremonial garb of their order, Magdalene and her apprentice, Tanara, stood sentinel and stoic behind Mary, Magdalene's hand upon her shoulder.

The soldiers, having grown impatient, turned to the women and the fallen.

"Your wailing will not bring him back from death," the head of the centurions growled. "He is gone, as you should be now, unless you require more need to cry, in pain and agony, as slaves to our whims."

The soldier began to slowly advance upon Mary, but at that moment thunder crashed and a shadowy figure appeared among them, seemingly from nowhere. The cloaked figure sliced between the soldiers, turned to the women and nodded, with a subtle gesture. Magdalene returned the gesture and she and her apprentice gathered Mary in their arms, leading her away, still a mess of sobs quivering in their comfort.

The figure watched them go, then turned to the centurions.

"Have you no respect for the dead and mourning?" the figure scowled.

"You shall find no mourning or respect for your dead body, if you dare to speak to us in such way again," the chief centurion bellowed. "Who are you to dare to do so?"

The figure removed the cloak from his head, and for a moment the men froze, startled at the Cimmerian steel of his gaze.

"I am Josephus, an Arimathean, and honored member of the Sanhedrin. I come to claim the body of my nephew, Jesus, for sacred burial in our family tomb."

"Under what authority? Your people hold no sway over the will of Rome."

The Arimathean reached into his robes and produced a scroll, which he handed to the man.

"Under authority of your governor of this region, Pontius Pilate, whose own seal decrees the body's release to me."

The centurion looked the scroll over dismissively.

"Very well, you shall have the body at tomorrow midday and not before."

"Why not now? Our customs dictate…"

"Your customs dictate little or nothing to us," the solider said. "We follow no law but that of Rome, and that of our own will."

The centurion pointed to the Sodomites' twisted figures, beginning to buzz and hover about the lonely body of the third dead.

"And of our own fortune," the soldier said, smiling, "as gained from them."

"Them?"

"The bodies are theirs, until tomorrow, at sun's apex, to do what they will. You shall claim yours upon this hill, then, or leave it to the beasts and vermin, but not before then."

The Arimathean slowly reached to his belt.

"I have silver, precious stones, gold…" he said.

"They have more," the soldier said. "They will always pay more."

The Arimathean reached once more to his belt.

"Not this time."

The Arimathean fixed his gaze upon the men, positioned himself between them and the fallen body of Christ.

"This body is mine, and I shall claim it immediately, along with all weapons of its destruction, all which pierced its flesh," he said. "In return, I offer you gold, or steel. Your choice."

"You dare to threaten us?" a soldier sniffed, incredulously.

"General, he is…" another soldier cowered.

"Quiet, you simpering, spineless fool," the general scoffed. "We are prepared for his kind. The charms around our necks will protect us from his Arimathean sorceries, and our blades shall see he joins his brethren in death and defilement this night."

The soldiers circled about him as the Sodomites lurked beyond them, hissing in delight as they anticipated the battle, as well as the bounty of fresh, unexpected dead.

"You come bearing Pilate's seal, so we offer you one final chance to leave your gold in our hands, your life in your own and the body yours at midday light," the general said to the

Arimathean, as the Roman unsheathed his sword. "This is your final chance to live."

"I come bearing the seal of the one true God so I offer you one final chance as well," the Arimathean said. "The body, mine, now, in exchange for the gold I offer. Your lives your own, hence forward."

"You had your chance," the general smirked.

"As did you," the Arimathean growled.

The soldiers raised their blades high, the steel slicing through the air, but the Arimathean moved with razor speed and clarity.

Dropping to a deep crouch he whirled about them, drawing his massive twin swords from beneath his robes and with two muscular, circular arcs, he sliced the soldiers off at the legs, his metal ripping straight through the bone, shearing muscle and sinew at their ankles and sending them tumbling, crying out in pain, crippled, to the ground.

Just as quickly, he pounced between them, and with a few quicksilver slashes their heads joined their feet, bloody and dis-attached from the dead meat of their torsos.

The Arimathean's gaze stalked about the killing grounds, watched as the Sodomites scrambled like roaches, fumbling for cover, away from his wrath.

Sheathing his swords, his mind leapt to the fields beyond, summoning.

Seconds later, a pale gray steed emerged from beyond, a cart trailing behind it.

Gently lifting the body of Jesus, the Arimathean laid it inside the cart, folding a billowing, violet cloak over it.

Then, looking over the grounds, watching as the Sodomites clung to the shadows outside his fury, he found the nails that had driven through Christ's flesh, the spear that had stabbed his side, and set them in the cart.

He glanced about the carnage, the slain, caked in dirt and blood. He heard the hiss of the Sodomites cowering in fear and anticipation, and slanting his eyes, his face a scowl, he gathered the bodies of the two men who had been crucified with Jesus, and likewise placed them in the cart.

Slowly, he climbed upon the horse, gazed once more upon the death about him, severed limbs and twisted bodies, then he looked to the skies, scarred charcoal and fire, and spurred the steed away, back into the darkness from whence he came.

And as he faded into the distance, the sound of hooves across the rocks growing dim, the slithering figures emerged once more. Creeping across the blood-soaked earth. Lurking with poisoned intent, over the fresh dismembered corpses of the soldiers, now silent, alone and helpless.

TWO

The flames rose high, licking the air with an ochre mist that was ripe with the cries of the tortured and dying.

Twisted bodies of the captured and slain were arranged in ritual fashion about the temple of Herod Antipas, their blood draining into a massive pit before them, decorated in demonic script to summon forth the denizens of hell.

The king sat smirking in delight and anticipation as he watched the summoning unfold. The sacrificed had been followers of the man who had fomented the slow-building rebellion, followers of the Christ. Not his inner circle of disciples, but those close enough to him that their auras still bore the halo of his presence, and their apprehension and execution would still make a clear statement to those who might think of an uprising in the face of Jesus' martyrdom.

Beside Herod Antipas on his right side was Lknng'tthr, his oracle, who empowered him in the realms of the dark magicks, and on his left side sat the Roman leader Pontius Pilate, the governor of Antipas' realm and of late his consigliore in the matter before them, the growing rebellion seemingly brought about by the ascendancy of Jesus Christ, a man who had appeared from relative obscurity only three years past. In that time, the Christ had stunned Herod's kingdom and galvanized a rapidly growing throng of believers with an amazing string of seeming miracles and claims of being the messiah.

Herod Antipas had studied the scriptures and knew well of the legacy of his father, Herod. He was well versed in the history of thirty-three years past, the alignment of the stars and the birth of the one heralded as the new messiah, the son of God. He was just as well aware of his father's attempts, both at that time and two years after it, to destroy or turn the infant, turn it to Antichrist, in order to finally overthrow Rome and rule the world. He had pored over his father's tomes, learned at the temples of the oracles and viziers, and was determined to succeed where his father had failed.

If indeed this man was the Christ, the one who had emerged three decades prior, Herod Antipas knew he would have but a short window to harness and usurp his power. He knew that the prophets wrote of his resurrection but three days from his death, and knew that the body of the Christ would be nothing but a hollow shell until that return. A shell that could be filled with darkness, reanimated, and repurposed as the Antichrist, to finally fulfil the destiny of the house of Herod, to hold the earth in his grasp, as the claw of Satan himself was used to slay and subjugate his enemies.

And so, on this Friday, as the stars held in alignment in the heavens, as the afternoon gloom of the storm oozed outside, the long-awaited plans of Herod Antipas began in earnest.

Within the palace temple the priests droned on, cloaked in black robes and the stench of incense burned along with the flesh of the doomed.

Wicked sigils, painted with the blood of the innocent, were arranged in cruel patterns about the floor of the temple, amidst the tableau of suffering and evil, and with each soul released in death, the dark gates' heaving maw above them, hovering, grew larger.

The reflections of the fires flickered diabolically over the steel of the centurions stationed about the temple walls, nimbly about the curves of their Roman armor, as it likewise illumined the robes of the priests and burned with vicious intensity in the eyes of the troika of men upon the throne dais.

At this same time the temple filled with malevolence, on the hill of the skull, Golgotha, not far from the king's palace, the Christ had been crucified, killed in ritual, upon a cross of unclean splinter, beneath the unholy sigil nailed above his head, a head pierced with a crown of thorns ripped and fashioned from a tree grown from the graves of six cursed men.

Above the murdering hill had hovered ravens, their eyes silvered. They were familiars, mirrors utilized by the black arts to see over vast distances, through their hollow orbs. And through those eyes, projected into the smooth globe of crystal before Herod Antipas, the king had seen the Christ call out one last time and breathe his last, mere moments before.

At the moment of his demise the sky had cracked with lightning and the earth shattered with thunder that rocked the temple and bathed it in an eerie green light. One which was drawn into a pulsing, awful fist of energy amidst the circle of sorcery before them, and which exploded, forming the gateway that now, now, opened up its gaping maw wider, wider.

The gateway was ripped open for the soul of the Christ, which had been sent to hell upon his body's demise. And it remained open, to birth the demons which would now come forth, led by the jagged form of Lucifer sent to inhabit the Christ body, as a zombie enslaved to the throne, to be sent into the world in a vulgar display of vengeance and power.

But then, just past the moment of Christ's death, the crystal went hazy, to be seen as nothing but a thick smoke within its glassy orb. Despite the efforts of the priests and vizier, it remained blank.

Lknng'tthr began to breathe deeply and a shudder crossed the vizier's flesh. His teeth gritted and he began to feel a sharp pain across his chest.

"Something is… wrong," the vizier hissed.

"It cannot be," Herod Antipas said. "All goes according to plan. The gate opens wide for Satan's arrival. The body is in the hands of the Sodomites, whose perversions will do nothing but ripen it for possession. And all others associated with the Christ will soon be in our hands, and then, they will be dead."

Herod Antipas called for his goblet to be filled and he drank deeply. And looking upon the spectacle before him, a cruel smile carved across his face.

"All is going according to plan," he said.

But unseen by the others, a ring upon Pilate's finger glistened a strange copper purr.

And above them, at the apex of the temple, hidden in the shadows, a raven's eyes glistened with the same faint copper patina.

Almost imperceptibly, Pilate glanced upward with a slight nod.

And with a silent thrust of its wings, the raven departed into the night.

THREE

History would write of them as mere followers.

But history is often little more than the plaything of its scribe, and oft times, the scribe has reasons to conceal, whether to make more mighty, or to make more humble.

They were twelve.

They did follow the Christ.

But they were more than mere acolytes in his shadow.

More than mere followers.

They were warriors.

A cadre of the skilled and courageous, trained by their elders, within the secret society of the Silent Hand.

A cadre put in place and picked through the intuition and precognition of the Christ.

A cadre to allow a man of peace a measure of safety to deliver a message of love in a world of hatred and war.

A magnificent array of guardians trained in the ways of the ninja, the arts of the sword and the craft of majick.

There were twelve. Eleven men, led by the mightiest warrior of them all, the woman, Magdalene.

And joined by one other.

One allowed to infiltrate their ranks as betrayer.

All as part of a clandestine plan known not even to all the disciples, known only to a select few closest to the Christ.

A plan unfolding about them as they remained in wait, placed in hiding, as the crucifixion took place.

During the public execution of their leader, Magdalene was stationed on guard, standing beside Mary, the mother of the Christ. As a woman, Magdalene would be seen to pose little or no threat, despite her innate clandestine power, and she, with her distaff apprentice, Tanara the Sin Eater, beside her, would insure the safety of the mother of Christ as she mourned her son.

The whereabouts of two other disciples, John the Revelator, and his brother in cunning and deadliness, James, together known as The Ones Who Walked Between Worlds, were unknown.

The treacherous Judas Iscariot had been expelled the night prior, after betraying the Christ and handing him over to the Romans for his public torture and death.

And so, ensconced in hiding, awaiting word of their next move from the Silent Hand, nine remained.

The Sons of Thunder: Simon Peter. The rock. The foundation. A warrior of vicious intensity, intellect and relentless attack. And his brother, Jude. A sly artist of the knives and brilliant mage with incredible powers of healing taught to him by the Magi Melchior himself.

Bartholomew. The Scorpion of One Thousand Stings. One of the finest archers in the kingdom.

Matthew. The Shadow Blade. A one-time apprentice of the Arimathean and a master spy and warrior, who, along with the Arimathean, had infiltrated the religious and political hierarchies of the time, providing valuable information for the rebellion.

Thomas. The All-Seeing Eye. Blessed with psychic vision and a brilliant swordsman.

Philip and Andrew. The Men Who Cheated Death. Brothers and former thieves. Experts in potions, deception and spells.

Simon the Zealot. A mysterious swordsman who spoke few words and brooked fewer still from his enemies.

James Alphaeus. The Cobra's Strike. A fearsome warrior skilled in the martial arts of the ninja, who could create a weapon of anything but remained as deadly without any weapon at all.

Together they had been assembled as a brilliant and fearsome force, an iron shield around a man marked for death from the time he had returned to his homeland.

They were with him at all times, brought together by the will of God and the machinations of the Silent Hand, trained in secret by the Magi of Earth's Realm.

The Arimathean.

The man upon whose signal they waited.

For the pinnacle of their mission, for which they had ultimately been assembled.

Waited.

Hidden away, in a secret room beneath an old shop once owned by Simon Peter's father.

Waiting.

"I am tired of waiting," James Alphaeus said.

"I am as well," Thomas said. "We wait while our leader is killed, wait for what, for Herod Antipas to find us?"

"We wait for our signal," Jude said. "For the Arimathean to summon us, when we are needed."

"When we are needed?" Bartholomew said. "We were needed when our Christ was tortured and slain! To stop his death or avenge it!"

"We are nothing but fodder for capture here," Philip said. "Herod Antipas' eyes are practically everywhere, and where they are not, Pilate's are just as wide. They have to know where we are at, and if they do not yet, they will shortly. And we are nothing but rats in a cage waiting to be flooded out underground."

"Perhaps, and perhaps not," Andrew said, contemplatively, noticing a look of discomfort jagging across Thomas' face. "Thomas, what do you see?"

"I see nothing, I have not been able to see anything since the Christ was taken," Thomas said. "But I feel… something… something not right."

Bartholomew turned to Simon Peter and Matthew, sitting silent at the head of the table.

"Perhaps it is merely my gut, but I feel something wrong as well," Bartholomew said.

"Perhaps it is because we were spotted, on our way here, when we were supposed to be careful," Philip said.

"That could not be helped," James Alphaeus said.

"James Alphaeus is correct," Matthew said. "We did what was right. What the Christ would have wanted us to do."

"It was a domestic dispute between a man and his wife, it was between them," Andrew said. "In all likelihood, she went right back to him after we stopped it."

"Or perhaps she did not," James Alphaeus said.

"Or perhaps, because of us, she was able to go anywhere other than to the grave," Matthew said. "He did not appear to be stopping until we stopped him."

"We did the right thing, she needed our help," Jude said. "We were placed in her path for a reason, and we could not turn away from that responsibility."

"But was it our responsibility?" Philip said. "I am not saying that what we did was not good, and not right, but we were in the midst of a crowd that could have helped but did nothing. Perhaps one of them would have if we had not. We were told not to hesitate, not to call any attention to ourselves on our way here, and we did, over a private matter. He was her wife, and by the old laws..."

"But did the Christ not say he was here to replace the old ways?" Matthew said.

"He said to respect them, to respect those that have come before, but to follow a new consciousness," Andrew said. "That is open to interpretation."

"The Christ followed no one," Simon Peter said. "He created his own path for others to follow. And there is no way the Christ would have not stopped that from happening."

"He would not have allowed it," Jude said. "The Christ considered all equal. Look at us. Look at those he chose to be his disciples. We are nowhere near royalty or elite. We are strange and ill-suited to this world. We are the people. And do not forget that among us is a woman, who the old ways would have seen as chattel, but whom the Christ chose as one of his greatest friends and allies."

"Jude is right, we are all equals in his eyes, man or woman," Simon the Zealot said. "He would never discriminate. Nor want ill to come to any. We were chosen to protect him, to follow him, to echo his ways."

He looked around the room.

"And he chose well."

"We did the right thing, we did the good thing to help that woman, we did what the Christ would have wanted done," Simon Peter said. "That is all that matters."

"But what if we were followed?" James Alphaeus said. "That other woman in the crowd, those two other men, they all identified Simon Peter. They knew he was a disciple of the Christ."

"And he denied them all, just as the Christ said he would," Jude said.

"But did they believe him?" James Alphaeus said.

Simon Peter shrugged. "We will find out."

Andrew and Philip looked at each other and then to Thomas and sighed.

"What do we do?" Philip said. "What do we do if we do not get the signal soon?"

"We will get the signal," Simon Peter said. "And it will be soon."

"And in the meantime, our leader is defiled and destroyed and sent to hell by the dark magicks of Herod Antipas and Roman sorcery," James Antipas said.

"As he told us he would be, James, remember," Matthew said.

Simon Peter stood and strode calmly around the room.

"Matthew is right," Simon Peter said. "It is all proceeding as the Christ said it would, as it was foretold."

"But why was he made to suffer so violently?" Thomas said, his head in his hands.

"Why do we weigh the dead to bury them at sea?" Jude said.

"What do you mean?" Philip said.

"The Christ was among us, but not of us," Jude said. "He was in human body, but he was not human, he was divine. As such, once he was released of the chains of human form, he would have been unable to fall to hell's domain. It was foretold that the Christ would unlock the gates of purgatory, travel to the bowels of hell, and save those souls held captive there. To do that, to be able to fall, his soul had to be weighed down, his body defiled in ritual. That is why it was allowed.

"Herod Antipas is a student of his father," Jude continued. "Thirty three years past, his father tried to capture the Christ as yet unborn and use his body as a shell, a powerful sheathe, for the sword of Lucifer, to turn him into the Antichrist. Once Jesus was born, he was unable to do that. Until now. Until the Christ was killed. And now, now that his body has been rendered hollow until his soul's return to it, Herod Antipas will once more try to fulfill the destiny his father so desperately attempted to see to fruition. He will try, in ritual, to fill the shell of Christ's body with the power of the devil to create Antichrist."

The disciples were silent.

"Then why are we apart from the body?" Thomas said. "Why did we not steal it away once it was slain?"

"It would have been too obvious for us to be there, waiting for its demise," Simon Peter said. "We had to let Herod Antipas think us unknowing, unaware, of its power and potential. He will let it slip, thinking it safe in the hands of the Sodomites as the Romans watch over them from afar, waiting for them to surrender it, even further defiled and readied for possession."

"Defiled?" James Alphaeus said. "How could that be allowed to happen?"

"It will not be," Matthew said, calmly. "As we speak, the Arimathean will retrieve the body, under guise of claiming it for family burial in his tomb."

"But how?" Philip said. "The Sodomites offer…"

"He will offer more," Matthew said. "Or, he will offer them no other alternative."

"Once the body is ours, we will accompany it into the desert, under cover of magick, and keep it hidden and protected until the third day when the Christ will once more inhabit it," Simon Peter said. "And then, when the world sees Jesus has risen triumphant, in accordance with the scriptures, they will recognize Him as the one, true Christ."

"And what if that does not happen?" Thomas said. "What if the Christ does not rise? What if he is like so many messiahs before him, who spoke of great destinies but ultimately were nothing but martyrs?"

"He said he was not, he said he was the one," Jude said. "So we either have faith in him, or we do not."

"If you lack knowledge, you fall back on three things: doubt, diligence or faith," Simon Peter said. "Only the latter two will keep you moving forward, seeking truth and knowing you will find it."

"We have been assembled for a reason, we are perhaps the finest warriors in this land, brought together by an elite organization, the Silent Hand, one which would not take such a matter lightly, nor one which would invest so much in a man who they did not feel was worthy of such effort," Matthew said. "We have all seen these previous messiahs, even some of great power, such as the Baptist. But only one displayed such power that he could be said to not only walk with the Magi, but to lead them. And that was Jesus the Christ. If he could perform those miracles, those great feats, how can we doubt he will be unable to perform this one?"

"But this is death," Thomas said. "Death. From which there is no escape."

"That is not true," Jude said. "There is escape from death."

The disciples looked to Jude.

"Among those sacred scrolls of the East, those brought forth by the Magi, there was written of a journey through death," Jude said. "A Kudi. A trek of three days' time, out of body, in which the soul could go through heaven or hell itself, but only if the journey was taken with the power of God in hand. A power which we have seen manifested in the Christ. If any among us, any of this earth, could take such a journey and survive it, we all know, from what we have seen, that it would be him."

The disciples were silent, sitting back in their chairs, contemplative, until Simon Peter spoke.

"We will all die, of that we are certain," Simon Peter said. "Whether the Christ returns or not, he has given us a gift. He has given us a cause to die for, a leader to follow. Whether we follow him in spirit or body, whether we lead a revolution of the heart or the fist, he has given us a cause. Something to live for, and something to die for. And when we breathe our last, we will know, now, that our lives have been worthy."

"Every man dies," Simon the Zealot said, "but not every man dies in glory."

The disciples nodded.

"We will have faith," Bartholomew said. "Faith in the path set out before us."

"Faith in the Christ," Jude said.

"And," Matthew said. "Faith in the ones who have guided us to this place, and who will lead us forward until his return."

"But, until then?" James Alphaeus said.

"Until then," said Matthew, "we wait."

James Alphaeus sighed.

Philip and Bartholomew grumbled softly.

The rest of the disciples sat quietly.

All but Thomas.

Gritting his teeth, he began to twitch, slowly, then with greater frequency, until he cried out and fell to the ground in pain.

"Thomas!" James Alphaeus said, rushing to aid his friend.

"Something is wrong," Bartholomew said. "Something is very wrong."

And as the disciples scrambled to help Thomas, there was a slight sound, heard beneath the din.

"Wait! What was that?" Matthew said.

"What?" Andrew said.

For a moment they were quiet, the only sound the heavy, feverish breathing of Thomas.

For a moment.

Silence.

And then,

At the door,

Something...

FOUR

An ivory owl wafted from the sky down among the three women in black robes, waiting at the massive stone tomb, and landed on the arm of the youngest of them.

She was taut and tawny, with the tiger's body of a warrior and a face tanned by the sun, eyes of exotic lands and stars of amethyst. She was possessed of a hard, ethereal beauty, a darkness that was a shroud, tight about her, yet one which, upon examination, seemed to hide a brilliant light deep within her.

Magdalene.

She looked into the owl's eyes, dark orbs reflecting the dim scraps of late afternoon sun barely visible through the mountainous clouds.

"He is here."

At that moment they heard the horse, the man with the carriage, and the body of the one they came to bury, and who they hoped, prayed, they would see once more alive.

Jesus.

The Arimathean arrived in a rush. The rain of the afternoon had dissipated and was now quickly being eclipsed by an oppressive heat as the clouds began to spread and the sunlight once more beat down upon the earth as evening cusped.

"Have you?" the man robed in dark with eyes of sienna and gold caught Magdalene's eye.

"Yes," she said.

"And all has been?"

"It has."

"Good."

He took the body of Christ clad in the purple sheathe in which he had placed it and held it tightly, gently, bringing it into the tomb. He removed the crown of thorns about its head, placed it in a white sarcophagus, said a prayer, and left it in the tomb.

He reappeared in the fading daylight, looking about the skies, scanning for any sign of familiars, black wings and eyes, waiting to act as the mirrors to their enemies.

He stood next to Tanara, as she awaited his signal.

Her eyes held no tears. Her angular face was a leathered visage of rugged grace, her body harsh and hardened, still bearing the marks, the healed scars of her youth, a youth condemned to the most wretched slavery, yet one freed by the man next to whom she stood.

Her heart was carved by what she had seen today. But she had seen far worse.

And even as the Christ's tortured body was carried inside the tomb and revealed, her eyes of burned sage had smoldered with a sadness, a resolve, a strength, for what she knew was to come.

One echoed in the eyes of the Arimathean.

The Arimathean, sensing all was clear, gestured to Tanara and she returned his sign, wrapped her cloak about her, leapt upon the gray steed, and parted, as Magdalene and the Arimathean stood guard.

And they watched and waited, a still in the air, tension pulled tight, waiting, waiting.

As inside the tomb, only one remained.

Mary.

Jesus' mother.

A few moments later, the two guardians heard a sound in the distance, a signal, of impending arrival.

James.

The Arimathean entered the tomb, sullenly, to find Mary weeping over the body. His head down, he put his hand upon her shoulder.

"I am very sorry," he said. "But we need to get you into hiding for the next three days, for your own safety. James will take you to a safe location."

"Just... can I?"

She looked down.

"Just for a moment," she said. "I just... want a moment, one more moment, alone, with my son."

The Arimathean looked to her, then down at the ragged earth, then to her face, her eyes, tearing, pleading, and he nodded, and left her alone with the body, laid gently into a lonely white stone sarcophagus, still covered with the violet cloak.

Then he walked out of the tomb, head down, to Magdalene, waiting for him, alone, as James had gone to gather water and other preparations for his departure and sequester with Mary.

Magdalene put a hand to the Arimathean's shoulder and he placed his hand over it, holding hers tightly.

"Is she?" Magdalene said, voice rising in sympathy.

"She is... as one would expect her to be," the Arimathean said. "After one has seen her son killed in such a way."

The Arimathean sat down on a large rock, next to Magdalene, and she put her hand on his.

She knew.

Knew his thoughts.

Without him saying a word.

Knew they were of his own children, his own wife, his own family, slain.

Killed while he was away on a mission with the Magi. Killed on the order of the previous king, Herod, father of Herod Antipas. Killed by Herod's other son, the half-demon Herodius.

The Arimathean still woke screaming at times, although the nightmares had grown less frequent, and she knew, without a word, the images that still burned in his mind. Of returning home to find the bodies.

"It is good Jesus' father was not alive as well to see this," the Arimathean said.

"A small blessing of his passing in peace," Magdalene said.

"He was a good man," the Arimathean said. "A good man. He and Mary were... very much in love... and he adored the boy."

"Yes," Magdalene said. "I remember them, as a child, and in growing older, when I returned to these lands."

They looked to the tomb, sat silent for a moment.

"I cannot imagine," the Arimathean said, "actually having to watch my child die."

He paused, breathed in heavily.

"It was… difficult enough to find them…"

He stopped.

His lips clenched.

Jaw tense.

"And yet," Magdalene said, nodding towards the tomb, towards Mary, "despite all, she remains more pure of mind and spirit, more filled with faith than us all."

"Yes," the Arimathean said. "All the more reason to protect her, and those like her, because the world would be a much poorer place without them."

Magdalene gazed into the distance as if looking, waiting, for someone to arrive.

The Arimathean looked to the shadows on the ground, measuring time.

"We should…" he said, but Magdalene's hand stopped on his.

"Let her have just a bit more time," Magdalene said, and looked into his eyes, the color of earth and sky married at day's end, hers echoing a lighter sienna of cinnamon and violet.

They sat in silence a while more, a strange tension in the air between them.

"What… do you mind me asking… what was she like? Your wife," Magdalene said.

"She was…not like me," the Arimathean said. "She was… she was kind."

Magdalene smiled. "You are kind."

"I am… not like her," he said. "She had a way, a smile under all circumstances. She used to sing… I would never… and her smile…"

He paused.

"She used to feed the birds that would fly by, and sit and watch them, quietly, content," he said. "I was always amazed at how it calmed her, at how content she was in this world with those small things so few of us would notice."

He breathed out heavily.

"One day… our son… he was… he was like me," the Arimathean said. "She was not outside, and he saw the birds collecting in the trees, and so he got his bow and shot one of the birds down. Not out of cruelty. For food. For us. For his family. He figured he was doing the right thing, like his father, he was providing us food. He was showing he was growing up, that he could. He thought it would make us proud.

"And it did… I was, I was proud that he would think of that," the Arimathean said. "He figured his mother had been clever, luring the birds into a trap so he could catch them for dinner. And, to be honest, I was very proud of him for being so cunning as to think that, and to want to provide, to help provide for his family.

"His mother understood too, and she did not say anything bad to him about it, she thanked him for hunting for the family," the Arimathean said. "But she also explained that she was not trying to trick the birds, that she had been being kind to them. That she had no reason for doing so, that she was just doing it because it was good to be kind, with no expectation of anything in return.

"And my son looked at her, the same way I had, so many times, just in… not disbelief, but almost beyond belief, like he, like I, could not comprehend what she was saying, what she was doing, because we had seen things so differently in our world.

"She could tell that, she could see it in his eyes, probably because she had seen it so often in mine, and she said to him, I will never forget what she said, she said that there is great ugliness in the world and it is easy to see because there is so much of it and it makes itself so loud and so vulgar. But there is also great beauty, if you just open your eyes to it, because it is more subtle and quiet.

"And she said to him, if more people, even those bathed in ugliness, would open their eyes to that beauty and embrace it, there would be a great deal more of it, and it would be far easier to see. And then she held him and told him that she saw the greatest beauty in his eyes, in the eyes of her children, and that she wanted him to know that he held that beauty inside of him and should never forget it."

The Arimathean looked out over the horizon, his eyes distant, misty.

"I had not heard words like that, thoughts like that again, until I met that woman," he said, nodding toward the tomb, "and again, until I heard the Christ speak."

He stood up, still looking towards the horizon, then to the shadows growing on the ground. Magdalene stood as well, nodded to him, and with a motion called her horse to her.

"That is why I do this," he said. "Because she would want me to, because maybe, if more people can begin to see the world like him, like her, this world could be a better place."

"More like him, and her," Magdalene said, looking into his eyes. "And less like you. And me."

The Arimathean averted his gaze, looked down.

"But then, perhaps, the world would not need those such as we," Magdalene said. "And we could actually begin to see the world as they do, and believe that it could be that way. And we could set our swords aside.

"Maybe we could learn to be more like them," Magdalene said, "because we could."

He kept his eyes to the ground for a few moments more, hoping to avoid hers, but when he looked up at her, as she readied to leave, her gaze caught his. And when he saw her, she was different somehow, different in her eyes, and his.

FIVE

The tomb was silent and much colder than the world outside it. A lone bar of light drew a path from the heavens to the white stone sarcophagus in which Jesus' body lay, cloaked in a violet shroud.

Mary took a moment to look upon it, partially in disbelief, partially in grief, partially, in a strange way, in thanks, as at least now, in death, her son was finally relieved of the violence and pain he had suffered earlier that afternoon during his torture and death by crucifixion.

He had told her of his destiny.

She had known, even before he said a word.

She had prepared herself, knowing what he, what she, would face.

But facing it was entirely different, and far worse than she ever imagined.

She walked slowly to the Jesus' side, kneeled down next to the sarcophagus, and it reminded her of years, decades, earlier.

Kneeling down, looking down, at this same body, so much smaller, still and sleeping, in his bed.

She remembered so many times, watching him sleep, looking at his face, marveling at its beauty, her heart bursting with love for this being which, it seemed, not too long before, was growing within her, moving about within her belly, as she and her husband talked to him, their hands moving across the ripe curve of her skin as he moved to the sound of their voices.

He was so much more, she knew, and, she knew, that this day would come.

But he was so much more to her, so much more, than he was to the world.

He was her son.

He was her life.

He was her love.

He was her baby.

Her little boy.

The one who spoke his first burbling words to her, who took his first steps into her arms, who hugged his little arms around her, in an embrace that grew stronger but no less tender and loving as years passed by.

She had remembered him, kicking inside her belly, felt him lulled asleep by the beating of her heart, a heart which always held him close.

Which still did.

So many times she had gently lifted a blanket over him, to protect him from cold.

Now, she softly removed the veil from his face, from a body already devoid of warmth.

At first she could hardly bear the sight, and her tears caught in her throat before erupting loudly in sobs, looking at the face of her son, beaten and cut and bloody.

But then she looked again, again, and her eyes didn't waver, and she saw, she saw, the marks drift away, the blood washed from his visage.

She saw, once more, the face of her beloved son, clean and beautiful, peaceful and serene.

She saw his smile, so often on his face.

His head tilted back in laughter.

His eyes, so full of love and wonder, so full of happiness, patience, knowing.

Knowing.

As they were the last time she looked into them, the last night he saw her.

The last night he talked to her.

Held her tight.

Kissed her forehead.

And told her he loved her.

And not to worry.

To never waver.

To have faith.

In God.

In Him.

I will see you again, he said.

You will look into these eyes.

I will hold you in these arms.

You must believe.

You must have faith.

In me.

In your son.

In God.

And so, through the pain and suffering, through the torture and agony, though the heartbreak and sorrow of having to watch him destroyed, her baby, her little boy, the one she held warm in her belly, on her breast, against her heart, whose hurts she kissed away as a child, whose hands she held and whose heart she felt most deeply, through all of those pages of life and love and pain, she had faith, despite having to watch him endure so much, so much.

So much.

So much.

But through it all, through her tears and pain and suffering for him, she believed.

She believed in Him.

She kept her faith.

And so, as she looked upon his face once more, looked upon this peaceful countenance that just moments before had been carved in pain, she smiled softly through her tears.

She leaned over, gently stroked the hair from his forehead, which still bore the marks of a crown of thorns removed just moments ago by the Arimathean.

She ran her fingers across his head, his hair, still wet with blood, just as it had been in his first moments of life, his first moments in her arms.

She leaned down to her baby's forehead, and put her cheek, her lips, to it.

And just as she'd done when he was a child, she kissed him.

"I love you son... I love you."

She lifted herself up, still looking down upon his face. She took a deep breath and let go of the tears, and through reddened eyes and pain, let herself smile.

"I will see you again... soon."

Then she reached down, touched his face once more, smiled, and turned, slowly, to walk away.

And just as she crossed the doorway, she turned, once more, and looked into the darkened tomb, let the tears run down her face, raised her hand as if to reach out to the son she was leaving behind, and in her heart, uttered a plea, a prayer, a dedication of faith, again and again.

"Please."

SIX

"What was that?" Matthew said.

"What?" Andrew said. "I didn't hear anything."

"I am sure," Matthew said. "I heard something. Just beyond the door."

"You heard nothing," Simon Peter said. "Be calm. We are safe. We have been assured. Only the knock of the one who will signal us will disturb us this night."

The disciples remained still, tense.

They listened.

Listened.

Nothing.

Only the sounds of Thomas, laying still on the floor, glassy-eyed and breathing with long, slow gulps of air.

"Who has assured you?" Bartholomew said.

"One we can trust," Jude said.

"We can trust no one," Bartholomew said. "At threat of their lives or those of their family, even the most virtuous can crumble."

"Or be seduced or overtaken by sorcery to force them to divulge our whereabouts," James Alphaeus said.

"Or merely asked to be pointed in the right direction, after we have carelessly betrayed our secrecy in public," Philip said.

Matthew looked to Thomas as Jude attended to him.

"How is he?"

"Better," Jude said. "He has calmed, and I am sure he will recover shortly. But we have seen him have these fits of prophecy before."

"Yes," Simon Peter said. "We have."

Jude exchanged a knowing look with Simon Peter, then Matthew.

"Then perhaps," Jude said. "We should be wary."

Simon the Zealot slapped a fist into his palm, angrily.

"I hate this! Hiding like rats underground, waited to be hunted down."

"And what would you have us do?" Matthew said.

"Fight! Rebel! Rise up!" the Zealot said.

"How?" James Alphaeus said. "The Christ is dead and even if he was alive a rebellion of steel was not among his plans."

"But he is dead, of that same steel, driven through his hands and feet!" Simon the Zealot said. "A week past his followers were legion. If we can rekindle that fire..."

"And how can we?" Bartholomew said. "Those followers are the same that chanted for his death just earlier today. They are sheep, a flock that does nothing but follow. And now, again, they follow Herod Antipas, they follow Rome, not the Christ. They do nothing but spit at his face. The same face they wanted to shower with kisses and smiles barely a week past."

"Wait," Matthew said. "There it is again! I am sure I heard it."

"I think I may have as well," Andrew said, leaning forward, his hand to his sword.

"Silence, then, silence..." Simon Peter said, raising a hand to the men.

The room was still as death, the air, musty and rancid, dust hanging, suspended as they strained to hear, anything, above the waves of Thomas' breathing, growing more frantic, frantic...

And then, in an instant, the door was smashed open and a fleet of Roman centurions were inside, swarming like wasps,

Roman steel flashing, centurions outnumbering the disciples four to one, with the Romans led by one most familiar to the disciples, a slicing, angular figure with clear eyes of black pearl and a face like a razor.

Judas Iscariot.

The disciples flared to battle, but were quickly cornered, overwhelmed in the small space by the massive wave of soldiers.

"We were ordered to bring you alive," Judas Iscariot said. "That is all which keeps you drawing breath at this time. You would be advised to relish your last moments of it."

Simon the Zealot exploded forward, sword in hand, towards Judas Iscariot, but for all of his strength and power, he was no match for the betrayer, who had been trained in the arts of death practically since his cursed birth. Judas smirked and laughed as he easily parried the Zealot's attack and disarmed him in seconds, leaving nothing but a red slice upon the Zealot's hand, which he drew into a fist to attack Judas. But once more, the betrayer dodged and parried, slamming a sharp elbow into the Zealot's face and knocking him unconscious.

The battle had taken but a few seconds and the disciples were stunned as their most fearsome and skilled warrior had been treated as little more than a plaything by the smirking Iscariot.

"Would anyone else like to try to amuse me?" Iscariot said, laughing.

Trading sideways looks, Philip and James Alphaeus raised their hands in holy magick, but Judas' eyes glared flame red and with a wave of his hand both men were thrown to the wall and collapsed to the ground.

Iscariot shook his head slowly, then sheathed his sword and crossed his arms over his chest.

Bartholomew, Andrew and Matthew began to advance upon Iscariot, weapons drawn, but Simon Peter stopped them.

"No," Simon Peter said. "Put your steel away. He has won, for now. Learn from the lesson of the Christ. It is less important to win the battle than it is to win the war."

"Yes, Simon Peter," Iscariot said in a mocking tone. "And sometimes you lose both."

The disciples sheathed their weapons and backed away as the soldiers advanced, slowly.

"Put them in chains and lead them to Pilate," Iscariot said. "They will join their leader in death by night's fall."

The Romans shackled the disciples.

But one would not submit.

Rousing to consciousness and grasping his sword, Simon the Zealot leapt towards Iscariot, but again, Judas reacted with deadly speed, dodging the attack and using Simon's momentum to shove him away to the ground.

"This is much less amusing than I thought it would be," Iscariot said.

Undeterred, the Zealot rose again, but before he could attack Iscariot once more, Judas' hand flashed to a pouch at his belt and two steel, spiked stars appeared in his hand.

The Zealot, dazed, bolted towards Iscariot, but nowhere near quickly enough. With a pair of blurs, Judas' steel shuriken zipped through the air, the first embedding itself in the Zealot's hand, causing him to drop his sword, the second chunked into his knee, forcing him to collapse again to the ground, unable to rise.

Two more stars appeared in Judas' hands. One ripped into the sword arm of the Zealot, the other into his sword, knocking it across the room and away from the disciple's grasp.

In a flash, Iscariot had grabbed the sword from the ground and stood over the Zealot, brandishing his own weapon upon him.

But instead of running him through, he smashed the side of the sword against the Zealot's temple, once more knocking him out.

Iscariot gazed with contempt upon the Zealot's body, then to the Romans, who were finishing up shackling the other disciples.

"Will someone get this scum chained so I do not have to waste any more time on his pitiful attacks?" Iscariot said. "I may become too tempted to kill him and I do not want Rome docking my silver at the expense of a corpse."

With the disciples in chains, the Romans led them out of the underground spot and into the oppressive heat and blinding sunlight of the fading day, the centurions at front and back of the beaten followers of Christ, Judas Iscariot at the rear of the procession.

The disciples were marched up and into a large cart drawn by two horses, soldiers surrounding them, as the other centurions mounted their steeds.

But not Judas.

He paused.

Looked around.

And then, with a quicksilver flash, he whipped his sword from its sheath, whirled and used it to smack away two silver shuriken which had been hurled at him from behind.

Iscariot smiled.

As a dark figure emerged from the shadows, twin swords drawn.

SEVEN

Judas Iscariot smirked as he looked upon the warrior stalking towards him, blades bared.

"Magdalene," Iscariot said.

"Judas," she scowled.

Iscariot pulled a second sword from its scabbard, filling both hands with steel.

"I was under orders to bring them in alive," Iscariot said, gesturing to the disciples. "But I have no such restraint in killing you."

"Nor do I, betrayer," Magdalene said, brandishing her swords.

Hoping to surprise her, three centurions, dressed in unorthodox Roman garb, similar to the ninja, but a bright red, leapt to confront her, whipping a half-dozen razor-sharp shuriken, metal throwing stars, at her.

However, Magdalene's Magi sixth sense had warned her of the attack a split-second before, and with lightning speed she spun in precise movements, using the armor wrapped about her forearms to deflect the stars back at her attackers. The steel missiles whipped back at them, into their soft flesh, sending their bodies crumpling to the ground.

Magdalene stood with her swords bared in a warrior's stance, looked at the bodies and then at Judas, with a smirk.

"Those things are dangerous," she said. "You should not have your children playing with them."

The other centurions bared their steel and began to advance upon Magdalene, but Judas, infuriated, waved them off.

"Go!" Iscariot yelled to the centurions. "I will handle this myself."

"They will go nowhere," Magdalene said, gesturing towards the horses to put them into slumber.

Iscariot laughed.

"They are enchanted and their reins are encrusted in Saturnari charms, immune to your Magi tricks," Iscariot said. "As are the soldiers."

With a start and a crack of the whip, the centurions sped off, the disciples enchained in the cart pulled behind them. Magdalene bolted towards the procession to halt it, but Judas quickly blocked her path.

"They will meet their end soon enough," Judas said. "But not as soon as you will meet yours."

With a flash he was upon her, his swords slashing through the air towards her in savage fashion, driving her back and almost pushing her to the ground, sealing her doom, but she whirled away and recovered, her own fire-hewed claws smashing against the steel fangs of her foe.

Iscariot would carry no nobility or honor in this battle, or any other, she knew, so even the slightest slip on her part would be met with a lightning-quick blade ripped through her. And then another, again, and again.

Judas Iscariot had been trained to kill practically since birth. An orphan, he was secretly taken in by Herod and the Romans and kept in luxury and decadence as he was steeped in the ways of destruction, trained in the ways of the diabolical, clandestine Roman warrior sect, the Saturnari, which steeped him in the deadly arts of combat and majick.

As an adult, he was released by his patrons and acted as a spy, infiltrating the growing rebellion in their land while waiting for his ultimate assignment, to act as betrayer to the Christ, once he re-emerged to take his place as a leader of men.

And so, he began to make himself known as an antagonist to the throne, to mingle with those who might find themselves amongst a rebellion, whether one of the body or the spirit.

Little did he know he himself was being watched.

Little did he know he had been destined from the start to betray the Christ, and that predestination was being utilized by the Christ and his followers to fulfill the prophecies.

The same prophecies Herod had, in his misguided way, sought to prevent from coming to fruition through Judas.

While the Romans and Saturnari used him as a weapon for their ends, in truth, Iscariot was nothing but a machine of death and consumption, caring for nothing but his own whims, his own appetites, and utilizing his skills as a killer to achieve them. In truth, his loyalties were to himself and his own depraved desires. He felt no conscience, no guilt, no compassion, no honor. And as such he would show none to Magdalene in battle or death.

He jabbed forward with one blade, forcing Magdalene to shift off balance and then followed with a volcanic swing that nearly decapitated her, but she was too quick, and all Iscariot's steel caught was the wisp of her hair, pulled back and tied, nipped by the razor-sharp edge of the sword that just missed licking her neck.

Judas cackled and continued forward on the offensive, measuring her strikes and parries and readying his claws for another potential death strike.

But Magdalene was once more up to the challenge, and her steel turned his away.

Within her, she exalted at slashing Judas back, and when she did, she saw those minute windows left open to attack him, and for that split-second, her blood was a volcano, longing to run her steel through him.

But she also knew those openings were a trick. A technique employed by the greatest warriors to trap opponents in their fever of emotion and overconfidence, get them to attack, get them off balance, get them in position to be ensnared and stung, shocked, then run through and slain. And so, she tried to remain calm, calculating, as the Magi and the Revelator had taught her, trying to curtail the cocktail of hatred and fear and anger within her. To fight with her head as much as her heart, if not more.

But the anger was almost too much. Especially with Judas.

During her time with the disciples, she had silenced her tongue and, as part of their greater plan, allowed herself to be diminished by Iscariot, to make him arrogant and overconfident. And so she endured his poison commentary and bigotry, his sexism and sense of entitlement. Just as the others had. Surrendering, allowing the Christ alone to cleverly and subtly contradict Judas, as he so masterfully did. Iscariot would not dare to contradict the Christ, not in an overt manner, and so when corrected, he fell in line behind him, at least to keep up appearances sake.

Men such as Judas had been a disease upon her all her life. They existed to keep her, and all women, in their place, as subhuman, as property, to be used and discarded and traded as they saw fit.

She had experienced this as a youth. Saw it in the death of her own mother, that left her an orphan, and in the abuse she had faced herself as a child until the Revelator adopted her, took her in, and taught her the ways of the Silent Hand, opened the doors for her to join in a community of equals, the Magi, where the accoutrements of the body held no meaning and true value was found in the spirit, the heart, the intellect and the desire of the warrior.

Men such as the Magi, the Arimathean, the Christ, held the hope of the future.

Men such as Judas, the subjugation of the past.

And so she could see it in Judas' eyes, as they battled, the disdain, the overconfidence. And so, she remained calm, feigned growing weakness, allowing his arrogance to grow, in hopes of exploiting it.

He smiled and a fire burned in his eyes.

For this victory, this blood, would have greater meaning.

This was more than just an assignment.

For Magdalene was more than any ordinary foe.

Like Judas, she was an orphan, adopted and trained in the arts of war and majick from a young age.

She had long been the apprentice of John the Revelator and later joined the Magi and Arimathean in their training among the halls of The Glowing City, S'iam B'ala, which hovered between the worlds.

In many ways they were very much alike.

But in the most integral, they were total opposites.

The most violent to Judas being that she was a woman, and therefore unclean and unworthy of her standing.

He had been raised to see her kind as little more than chattel, property, to be used as he and all men saw fit, and disposed of accordingly.

He found it disgusting that the Magi, and the Christ, held such pagan and perverse views. He thought it blasphemous and repellent that they not only considered women equals, but would consider them capable of even greater achievements than men, and educated and trained them as such, allowing them access to the same advantages as those who should be ruling them.

Again he slashed Magdalene back onto her heels and once more he thrust forward, this time with an explosive strike which would have run her through and buried his steel fist deep into her.

However, once more, she eluded death.

He was amazed at the skill Magdalene had shown as a mage and warrior.

But he had no respect for it.

He saw it as little more than a curiosity, an aberration.

One which he would now destroy, to prove his superiority.

As his blades slashed about her, amidst his relentless and calculating attack, he imagined what he might do with her, with her body, once he had slain her, and how he might keep it as a trophy, to display to the disciples, before they were led to their deaths.

His mind pooled with his poison.

His lips curled sardonically.

And he began to weary of this battle, began to think of its finish, to relish her death.

And so he began the sequence of blows that he was certain would lead to her demise. The series of jabs, slices and parries that would leave her completely open and vulnerable to his blade, first stunning her, then crippling her, then finally impaling her through and down, down to the ground before him, bathed in her blood.

But...

He could not.

His steel slashed away, more and more intensely, but at every move, she countered.

He began to grow ever more frantic.

Ever more angry.

And then, as if she could sense his frustration, her counters began to be joined, by counterattacks.

Not only was she parrying his attacks, but she was matching them and sending her own blade closer, ever closer, to his own flesh, until, as his frustration sent him off-balance just the slightest bit, her blade caught the cusp of his cheek and for the first time of his adult life, Judas Iscariot felt his flesh rent by the steel of another, felt his own blood sting and flood warm down the sweat of his skin, and felt something he had not felt in years, if ever.

He felt...

Fear.

He tried to beat it back, tried to lash it down deep inside him, but it seeped from behind its restraints, like tentacles of doubt into his mind and heart.

Fear.

Of her attacks.

Of her steel.

Of her.

Of the humiliation of being defeated.

By her.

Of failure.

Of... death.

His attacks continued, all the more furious, his swords smashing against hers with greater intensity and frequency, but again and again, he was countered. And then, once more, her steel slashed his skin, this time across his forearm, stunning him for just a moment, but more than enough time for her to send what could have been a killing blow towards him, if not for his superhuman reflexes.

And then, the tentacles began to creep up all the more, the fear began to well up inside him, to fill him up, and he could feel it, alien and toxic, could feel himself falling back, no longer attacking, but defending himself, as she became the attacker.

She.

Her.

A woman.

Defeating him.

The most deadly warrior upon the earth, he thought.

But, maybe...

Maybe not...

And as the fear began to overtake him, the voices began inside his head, strange voices he had never heard before, the cackle of evil accompanying them, echoing through his mind, until he could no longer hold on.

With a long, violent swing of his blade, he created separation between the two of them, sent her back into a defensive stance.

It was more than enough space.

He quickly grabbed the black powder from his belt, scattered it to the ground and air between them and it erupted in flame.

She hurtled back several feet through the air as she had been trained, landing on her feet, blades up, expecting the distraction to lead to him bursting through the wall of flame with renewed attack, expecting sorcery to accompany his steel, and readying herself to battle him with her own majicks.

But as the smoke dissolved and the flames folded ashen to the ground, she saw… nothing.

He was gone.

Retreated.

Escaped.

She scanned the area, expecting a surprise attack.

But it did not arrive.

It would not arrive.

Judas Iscariot had run from her.

She had faced the deadliest warrior of her enemy.

And she had survived.

Survived on her skills, on her wits, on her body and mind.

But she would not consider it a victory.

For she stood alone.

Without those she had come to retrieve, those she had come to lead.

So, she called her steed.

And she rode off, back into the heart of the city, to find her destiny.

EIGHT

The two shrouded their faces and bodies as they moved through the crowds.

James held his arm around Mary, protecting and guiding her. The Arimathean had warned them well of the danger inherent in anyone discovering their identities. Until sunrise on Sunday chaos and unpredictability were the only certainties in their world.

James knew well how the whims of the crowd could turn quickly in deadly fashion. Mary may well have been ignored, on this and the rest of her days, but just as probable would be the possibility that at one glimpse, one condemnation, the crowd would swarm her. Not to mention that it was almost a certainty, the Arimathean said, that darker, more sinister forces would attempt to kill her or kidnap her, for more unspeakable reasons.

She still bore the blood of the Christ, still remained a tie, an altar, for the potential creation of his being, a link to the higher world. And those of supernatural ilk would be intrigued by the possibility of discovering just how that power, that potential, could be utilized to their advantage.

During these dark days, with the Christ having descended to purgatory and hell, his body nothing but a hollow shell, in danger of being overtaken by the forces of evil, they were all in danger, and they knew those arrayed against them would stop at nothing.

They knew, they were well studied in the writings and the stars, the alignments placed by God. And they revealed that this world would stand on the precipice between good and evil, on the brink of chaos, for this time with the Christ descended, and then would not be as ripe for conquer again for another 2000 years. If Satan was to achieve his goal of completely devouring this world and creating hell on earth, completely expelling God's influence and power upon it, the time was now, within this window.

And so, Mary would be hidden, until that fateful sunrise, on the third day.

The two tried to cover their tracks, tried to take an odd and oblong route to their place of refuge, to shed any potential pursuit, clandestine or otherwise. Finally, they came to a small, unassuming dwelling. James looked around, then knocked in a strange, staccato fashion. A signal to those inside.

Silence.

Again, James knocked.

And in return, instead of a countering set of knocks, as expected, the door merely opened, slowly, and a familiar voice rasped from behind it, "quickly, get inside."

James was gripped with cold.

The Arimathean had been quite clear.

They had been told to knock in a specific pattern.

Another pattern would be returned.

And if it did not, they had been compromised, and were to flee, to another location.

James looked to Mary, then whispered in her ear.

"Get behind me," he said, "stay with me, we must go."

He pulled his sword, as they turned to flee.

But it was too late.

The door flung open, and the body of the man they had been told to meet, Jeremiah the Wanderer, was hurled towards them. His throat slit. His mouth silenced.

James grabbed Mary and turned to run, but surrounding them were a cadre of Romans, armor glistening, swords drawn.

The two turned towards the door, and through it, flanked by soldiers, was the sneering countenance of a stout, heavy man, clad in the dark robes and headgear of the Sanhedrin.

Caiaphas.

"So," the high priest purred in an oily voice. "We meet again."

The soldiers drew steel but James was quicker, lacing through three of them before they could even thunder their weapons against his own.

But Caiaphas knew well the power of the brother of the Revelator. As well as his weakness.

James was stung from behind by the lash, turned to defense it, but was slashed by another, felt the blood well from his cheek, and the slow venom in which the lashes had been drenched.

The oil of nightshade.

Like a pit of vipers, they were suddenly slashing at him as he whirled his steel about, with superhuman reflexes, slicing the lashes to worthless bows of leather as they whipped toward him.

But they were too many.

The sweat and heat of the poison made the world spin and wobble about him, dropping him to his knees.

"Finish him!" a centurion bellowed, sword raised.

"No!" Caiaphas said, holding out a beefy arm. "He is wanted alive, to face the arena!"

The centurions threw nets about the body of James as he struggled to maintain consciousness, the poison racing through his veins counteracted only by his training, his spirit, the unquenchable will fired in the secret temples.

Another Roman grabbed Mary, who cried at the sight of James captured.

"And what of her?" the soldier said. "She is to be left alive, but in what condition?"

"Keep her in line at sword's point, but leave her untouched," Caiaphas said, with a smirk, "for now."

NINE

The sound was brief but unmistakable, breaking the silence and dim of the palace dungeons.

Steel on steel.

The sharp shard of conflict.

Then, a pale gurgle, a weak thump and an enveloping quiet once more.

But enough. Enough to rouse the men, within their cells, to bring them to crane themselves to attempt to see outside.

Another wet gurgle. Another crumpled collapse. The sound of dead flesh falling to the dirt.

And another. And another.

And one more quick slash of steel clanging, more loudly than the last, a muffled cry and again, the cut strings dirge of a body dropping, dead.

Then, silence.

Silence.

In their cells, the disciples zipped about, their eyes darting through the steel bars, until a figure, sheathed in black, emerged at the door, rapidly picking their locks with expert ease.

"Quickly! Follow me! I am here to free you!"

The men moved hastily out into the hallway, following the figure.

"Wait!" Thomas said. "Who are you? Why are you here? How do we know you are not leading us to our deaths? How do we know for sure you are here to save us?"

The figure halted, kicked the body of a dead guard.

"Ask them your last question!" the figure said. "Now hurry! The sounds of steel echoing once may not rouse those above, but the repeated sounds of swords in battle could certainly cause suspicion to become action."

"But who are you?" Philip asked.

The figure pulled his cowl aside for a moment, revealing a face, worn, rakish and familiar.

"You!" Matthew cried out.

"You have much to answer for!" Bartholomew came at him, only to be pulled back.

"And I shall, later, after we leave this place! Follow me!"

The figure led the disciples up through the catacombs in quiet haste, up the stairs and through the prison, past the bodies of those he had slain to get to them, until finally they reached the main gate.

He turned to the men as he pulled a bow from the back of his cloak and shifted it aside, revealing a full cowl of arrows.

"Once through, follow me and run like lightning. I will cover us if need be, but we should face little resistance. Most of the guards are drunk and sated, figuring the movement is crippled, and those who had the misfortune of being here are dead by my sword. We should find it easy running to the hills and into hiding where we will rendezvous with those who will help us on the next of our mission."

The apostles nodded in agreement and began to carefully shuffle through the exit way, as their liberator loaded two arrows into his bow and struck it back, pointing it towards enemies he hoped would never come.

They pushed through the door and into the courtyard to see little but the corpses he had left behind, nothing but bodies bleeding death and the vast array of stone pillars leading to the entrance.

The figure dropped his guard, slightly, his bow moving just ever downward. He let out a deep breath.

"As I said, our way is clear," he said. "Now quickly, follow me!"

He grasped the bow and arrows in his hand and began to lead the men as they ran towards the hills beyond the outskirts of the city, but as they passed the last pillar they heard a sound, a crack, behind them, and turned to see the lash strike at the back of Thomas to the end of their pack, sending him screaming to his knees.

And they watched as the soldiers emerged from behind the pillars.

Heard once more the crack of the lash from the remnants of the city before them, and saw as Simon Peter fell to the ground in agony, quickly enveloped by another group of centurions.

Within moments they were surrounded.

"Drop your arms or die now!"

The figure's body slumped and his bow and arrows fell useless to the ground, followed by the swords from about his waist.

The group of soldiers before them parted, and a white horse emerged, stopped, and the robed, crowned figure upon it slowly dismounted.

With a wicked smile, flanked on both sides by a pair of centurions, the king, Herod Antipas, walked towards the once-more captured disciples and their would-be liberator, his face still shrouded.

Herod Antipas chuckled and approached the men with mock sorrow.

"Ohhhh, it would appear your attempts at escape were so sadly short-lived," the king said. "But such a valiant effort, and very amusing for us to witness, such entertainment, such a prelude, to what we hope to expect within the hour, as you enter the arena!"

Herod Antipas stalked about them, before drawing in close to the masked figure.

"Yes, the people are very excited, especially after this afternoon's crucifixion, to slake their growing thirst for blood," the king said. "We had already rounded up a significant number to face the beasts and blades. But the blood of these followers of the criminal executed will make for a very pleasing addition. And I would venture to guess the crowd will be even more excited to watch as we unveil for them a most unexpected twist, a new condemned, doomed to be executed, enemy of the state. Especially one which had so soon before, so ironically, escaped the same fate."

Herod Antipas stepped to the figure and ripped the cloak from his face.

"Do you not agree," Herod Antipas smirked, "Barabbas?"

TEN

Thirty-three years earlier, just prior to the birth of Christ, the ruler at the time, the insidious King Herod, had attempted, with the help of Satan, to slay the Christ's parents and rip out the unborn baby to try to turn it into the Antichrist and rule the world.

Despite unleashing a virulent plague of demons, led by Herod's own half-succubus son, Herodius, they failed in their plans, thwarted by the combined might of the three Magi – Balthazar, Gaspar and Melchior – and the mysterious Arimathean.

However, two years after the birth of the Christ, the stars aligned in the Mark of the Dragon for a brief, but violent, time, allowing the chance for the child's destruction and the unleashing of hell on earth.

Knowing this, having been alerted to it by Satan, King Herod ordered a purge – the slaughter of all male children under three. But in truth, the soldiers enacting it were far from

discriminating. Children of all ages were destroyed, many of
them after being defiled and debased as their parents were forced
to watch or be killed themselves in daring to attempt to protect
their beloved offspring.

The Arimathean had known of this time as well. And
although he had pledged to remain in protection of the youngling
Christ, along with the other three Magi, he could not ignore the
suffering.

Because almost a decade prior to that point, he had lost
his own to it.

He had once belonged to the order of the Magi, a warrior
of the Secret Hand.

Balthazar had summoned him, on a mission involving
the birth of a new child, one who would be called The Baptist,
who the prophecy said would prepare the way for the Christ.

The Arimathean followed the Magi on their mission.

He left his wife and children behind, thinking them safe,
holding and kissing them farewell, for what would be the last
time.

When he returned, it was to the news of their deaths.
Some of their bodies could not be found. Others, unfortunately,
were.

At that point, he turned his back on God and humanity,
until finally being recruited back into the Magi by Balthazar, to

safeguard Mary and Joseph, the parents of the Christ, and, to ultimately get his revenge on the half-man, half-demon which had slain his family, Herodius, the son of Herod.

But while his sword had slaked itself on the blood of the beast who had destroyed those who ruled his heart, it hadn't so much as tasted revenge against the one who had in essence ordered their deaths through his own fear and paranoia.

King Herod.

The same man who was ordering the murders of children and families two years after the Christ's birth, for ostensibly the same reasons.

And so, leaving the three Magi behind in defense of the infant Jesus and his parents in Egypt, the Arimathean returned to Jerusalem, to stop the bloodshed, to gain some measure of peace. For if he could not bring back his own family, his own children, at least he could prevent others from suffering the same fate.

His battles were valiant, legendary, but ultimately futile. He was one man, a leader or follower of none. For all he saved there were countless others he did not, could not save.

And when the cost of blood had become too much, when the sight of pain and suffering had poisoned him, he found himself compelled, a fire within him, to leave the dead behind and to seek out the living, who had condemned the slain, needlessly and selfishly, in their hunger for power and their paranoia over losing it.

It was dusk, with darkness just passing over the horizon like a funereal shroud, when the Arimathean attacked.

He had spent a week analyzing the defenses of the palace. He spent the day preparing. The nights were lax and debauched, with Herod engaging in perversions and rituals and his exterior guards often lazy and drunk. It was quick work to eliminate them, arrows slicing the air in a torrent of destruction, silent and decimating, not alerting those inside. And so his path into the palace, and out of it, was clear.

The elite guard inside would be another matter.

Battle-hardened and protected by sorcery, they were the finest warriors of the kingdom.

The finest, save one.

Him.

Arrows would only dispatch so many before their attentions would quickly focus on the attacker and so, after death had rained from above, eliminating over a dozen men in an instant, the Arimathean shattered a crystal of mystification upon the marble floor and leapt from his perch, dropped down among them, his heightened senses enabling him to seek and destroy as they hopelessly flailed about, powerless to his superior magicks.

When his twin swords had devoured their share of blood and flesh, and the floor was scarred with the lives of Herod's would-be guardians, the Arimathean dismissed the mists with a wave of his hand, leaving the room lit only by the candles lacing the walls.

There, simpering and shrinking behind his throne, was the sweaty, drunken mess of Herod, shouting for his vizier.

The Arimathean strode towards the throne, but before he reached it, Herod's vizier, V'kk'nithr appeared before him, as if from a black ether.

A bolt of crimson energy ripped from the wizard's hands towards the Arimathean, meant to burn him in unholy fire, but it was for naught. In a blur, the Arimathean unsheathed an ivory scabbard from his belt and a fang of blue flame emerged from it, not only deflecting the attack but crystalizing the energy bolt and disintegrating it into dust, instantly blown to a breeze that whipped through the palace, straining the candlelight and lashing the robes of the wizard.

Upon seeing the bright blue blade of fire, V'kk'nithr's face drained pale.

"Soulsfire…" the dark mage muttered in terror as he beheld the holy sword of S'iam B'ala. "Lord of Darkness, help me!"

"He cannot help you now, nor will he," the Arimathean growled, as he leapt to the throne and with a mighty swing of the holy sword, disintegrated the half-demon body of the vizier, his death shrieks echoing as his tar-dark soul was sent to hell and his human shell fell to a pile of smoldering ash upon the ground.

The Arimathean turned, sheathing the holy sword and once more filling his hand with earthen steel.

"And now, Herod, it is time for you to pay for your crimes against your own people," he said, hurling the king's ornate throne aside and looming over the cowering man, frightened and skittering, like a cockroach upon the ground.

Their eyes met. Herod's black as a sharks, but pooled with fear. The Arimathean's barren earth, merciless and cold.

"My God," Herod babbled, "I remember you."

"And I, you," the Arimathean said.

"What have you become?" Herod pleaded.

"What you have made me."

"Why…"

"Why?" the Arimathean smirked with disbelief. "You disgust me, you parasite, you harlot of Rome. You destroy your own, a slave to nothing but your depraved desires and perverse thirst for unending power. You deserve to rule nothing but the dirt as the vermin eat away at your dead flesh, as the demons suck away the meat of your soul in whatever hell you infest for eternity."

Herod summoned up a vestige of courage and defiance and spat towards the man looming over him, but the sputum fell back onto the king's robes, deflected by the Arimathean's magicks.

"You dare to judge me?" Herod said. "Whatever hell I reach you will soon join me. You are too stained for heaven, for the depth of blood on your hands rivals mine and is just as red."

"Your God will turn His back on your soul, one as poisoned as yours," Herod sneered. "Only Satan will embrace you with open arms and fangs to neck."

The Arimathean raised his sword.

"Well then, give him my regards."

With one powerful swing, he sent the head of the king sailing across the throne room, as Herod's body fell limp to the floor, red pooling quickly upon the white marble.

The Arimathean paused.

A sound.

Small and whimpering.

He girded himself against another attack, swinging around to catch its direction.

A scratch.

A muffled cry.

He saw a blur, a body, bolting from behind a curtain.

With one outstretched hand in its direction, one sorcerous burst of power, he stopped it cold, and the fleeing figure froze.

He was quickly to its side.

It was a boy. From the looks of him barely on the young side of puberty.

Dressed in royal garb.

Herod's son. Heir to the throne. Herod Antipas.

The boy was thin and weak-looking, with barely a hint of the harsh, foreboding countenance of his father.

The Arimathean knew, he had seen, he had experienced, that age or appearance had nothing to do with how deadly or evil an opponent could be.

But there was something frail, something sympathetic about this child, something that led the Arimathean to stay his sword.

Stay it, but not sheathe it.

With the boy still frozen in a supernatural grasp, the Arimathean raised his blade to the neck of the soon-to-be-king.

"Your life is in my hands," the Arimathean said, "and it always will be. If you follow the ways of your father, you will likewise follow him in death."

The boy nodded, frightened.

"Your power is a responsibility, just as mine is," the Arimathean said. "We are your people. Jerusalem is in your blood. Not Rome. So be careful when you choose to spill this country's blood, for you will be spilling your own."

The Arimathean lowered his sword and released the boy from his grasp.

"Go, and hope you never look into my eyes again," the Arimathean said. "For it will be the last time."

The young Herod Antipas, quivering in terror, nodded quickly and backed up, eyes still transfixed on the man, before turning and quickly running off into the palace.

The Arimathean sheathed his sword. Took one more look around the room.

Again.

The sound.

He paused, once more, to locate it.

Froze a few seconds, then darted to a strange stone coffer on the dark side of the throne room. It was an egg-shaped receptacle, completely sealed but for a few strange slits along the side, from which the sound emanated. Carved into the egg were occult sigils and ritual spells which were likewise curved about it on the floor, written in blood.

The Arimathean wrapped his powerful grasp around the lid of the object and pulled it off with a heave, to see what Herod had intended to sacrifice for some diabolical ritual.

The sight sickened him and made him feel both revulsion and satisfaction in having killed the king this night.

A male infant, no more than a few weeks old, lay in the sarcophagus, naked, in a shallow, warm pool of blood and silver pieces. The baby, obviously weakened and malnourished from its appearance, was practically too weak to cry out, its only means of protest a series of anemic moans.

The Arimathean took his cloak from his back, wrapped the baby in it and cradled the infant in his grasp, holding it tightly to his chest as he clutched steel in his other hand, and quickly strode from the palace and into the night.

He got onto his horse and rode to a distant town, one from his prior travels.

There, he met a couple, whose five children had all been massacred at the hands of the marauders. The man and woman had been horribly scarred and injured, but had survived and healed almost completely by the grace of God.

Almost, but not completely, as they remained barren. Barren, but longing.

They wept tears of joy as the Arimathean explained to them what had happened, how he had saved the child and how he had remembered them, remembered their devotion, and thought they would best provide a safe and loving home for the unknown child.

The woman held the baby close as the man went to retrieve it fresh milk and clothing.

"He is a blessing from God, as are you," the woman said, tears washing down her cheeks, as she looked at the Arimathean with happiness. "We will never forget you. Never."

The Arimathean nodded, humbly, in appreciation.

"Please, allow us to have you in our home, for a meal, for shelter, should you need rest," the man said.

The Arimathean smiled slightly, but shook his head.

"I thank you, but I cannot," the Arimathean said. "There are too many suffering in this land and my time here is short. I cannot rest."

The couple nodded. "We understand," the man said, "but know we are forever in your debt, and you shall always be welcome here."

The woman held the baby up, looked at him under the moonlight, the infant now asleep and warm, a sanguine calm over his small, wrinkled face.

"He is beautiful," she said to her husband, "is he not, Jeremiah?"

Her husband nodded and smiled.

She looked at the child, and then to the Arimathean, and then to the child again.

"He has come from shame, but shall be raised in glory and love. He will be brought up to be a follower of none and a leader of many," she said. "And we shall call him… Barabbas."

ELEVEN

The clouds dissipated, the air of the evening still oppressively humid, the arena was a whirlpool of sweat and bloodlust, as the crowds drunkenly cheered the grisly deaths raining red upon the dirt and sand.

Protected in a stone enclosure open over the arena, Herod Antipas and Pilate, flanked by guards and servants, drank deeply, of wine and blood, as they laughed at the spectacle of those doomed to die and those watching whose own lives were little more than a different sport to men of power.

And deep within a cavern opening up to the arena, twelve men in chains were being led, to the lip of its gaping maw, to the scalding burn of the sunlight.

"At least we die on the day of our Christ," Matthew said.

"And with him in heaven we will be tonight," James Alphaeus said.

Barabbas sighed.

"Oh, how ironic," Barabbas said. "That ye of so much faith display so little."

"This is nothing you can thieve your way out of, Barabbas," Thomas said. "You cannot steal from death."

"I disagree," Barabbas said, "as I have stolen my life back many times."

"Only the Christ has the power to steal his way from death," James Alphaeus said.

"You would do well to ask for forgiveness for your sins while you can, Barabbas," Philip said.

"I would if I had any to forgive," Barabbas said. "Alas, I find myself short."

"You are a thief, same as my brother and I," Andrew said. "The laws say…"

"The laws," Barabbas scowled. "The laws are what imprison us now, you fools. The laws are little more than the legitimized corruptions of corrupt men."

"Not all men are corrupt, nor are all laws," Matthew said.

"But it does not take all, only a few in the worst places of power," Barabbas said. "The well may be filled with a sea of water, but it only takes a few drops of venom to poison it."

"The Christ offered refuge from that venom," Jude said.

"The Christ offered a new well, from which to drink," Barabbas said, "But before those can make their way to his well stream, they needed an antidote for the water they drank which was already poisoned. I offered that.

"People can fill their mouths with words like hope and change, but they cannot fill their bellies with mere words," Barabbas said. "I steal from those who have gained their gold through a more insidious theft, the kind made legal by the politicians they have bought. And I give to those whose needs should come before the wants of those with already too much. I did so before the Christ, during his leadership, and will likely continue to do so after.

"And yet you stand alive before us, while he is dead," Andrew scowled. "You were the one chosen by the crowd, when they were asked if you or the Christ should be slain, when you know you were far guiltier and deserving of death than he was or ever will be."

"As it was written, as he himself said it would be," Barabbas said. "You are right. He was, he is, a great man, far greater than I will ever be. And I would have gladly given my life for his. He is worth more dead than I am alive. But that was not to be, and you all know it. I stood before Pilate, I stood before the crowd, beside him, and the crowd was given the choice to kill me or kill him, and they chose the Christ."

"So it was written that they would," Matthew said, looking around at the others. "Barabbas is right. We cannot hold a grudge against him for the whims of the crowd which chose the Christ for death and Barabbas for freedom. It was not Barabbas' choice, and the Christ himself said it would happen. He said he would die. And he said he would also rise. We need to have faith in him."

"And we also need to have faith in ourselves," Barabbas said.

"And what faith should we display?" Thomas said.

"The faith of long lives, or at least those beyond this arena," Barabbas said. "We are not dead yet."

"Yet," Andrew said. "But very near the precipice of it."

"I am not afraid to die," Bartholomew said.

"I am not either, but I would prefer to remain among the living if at all possible," Barabbas smirked.

Jude walked to the fore with Barabbas.

"Barabbas is right," Jude said. "While we still breathe, we still have faith, we still have hope, and we still survive."

A massive centurion laden in armor jabbed a spear towards them.

"You survive at the whims of Herod Antipas," the soldier said. "And not for long."

The Roman watched the killing grounds as the last of the previous field of sacrifices was ripped apart by lions.

"Say your final prayers, to your God who never answers them," the soldier scoffed.

Barabbas turned quickly to the man, who jolted a bit at the advance, before righting himself.

"He never answers them for you," Barabbas said.

Within the arena, the keepers leashed the beasts once more, the warriors sheathed their weapons and backed to the arena's edge, and the killing floor was once more devoid of anything but mangled parts and corpses, and disgusting jags of blood and gore slathered about.

The crowd roared in anticipation of the main event, and Herod Antipas smirked and turned to Pilate beside him.

"When the people's minds are filled with sex and horror, their souls breed little but greed and fear," Herod Antipas said, "and both are intoxicants that allow for a populace more easily led."

The crowd noise buzzed loudly. Trumpets stabbed the air calling them quiet as Herod Antipas rose to greet them.

"Oh, my loyal subjects, we have such a great treat for you tonight," he began, laughing, as the crowd roared in appreciation.

"As you know, today we executed three criminals of the state, whose crimes and sedition against your way of life were well documented," Herod Antipas said. "And now, tonight, you will witness the execution of their accomplices, their partners in crime, whose disgusting acts and traitorous rebellion have been well documented and will now be punished for the good of the state!"

Simon Peter shook his head.

"My father told me of this place when I was growing up, I remember him speaking of the last Herod and his bloodlust," Simon Peter said. "I remember him being hopeful when he was killed, thinking Antipas might be different in some way."

He chuckled sarcastically.

"We soon realized that was not the case," Simon Peter said. "We exchanged one Herod for another, barely less brutal and psychotic due only to his own incompetence. I hardly call that progress."

The crowd exploded in a frenzy, howling and whooping for blood.

"People get the leadership they deserve," Thomas said.

In the entryway to the arena, Thomas watched in disbelief and disdain.

"It was but a week ago, these same people were cheering and howling for Christ's entry into this city, with us at his side," he said. "Now they cheer for his death, and ours as well."

"So easy then, to say, they are not, and never will be, worth it," added Bartholomew. "We would have been well off to use our lives and energies elsewhere, and Christ as well."

Barabbas shook his head slowly.

"You are wrong," Barabbas said. "People are sheep, living in fear, waiting to be led. They follow along because it is easier that way and because they believe they have no choice. Even if they feel differently, they dare not risk being ostracized for standing out in the crowd. To condemn these weak fools for anything other than that is to condemn a herd for running in unison from a lion or a flock of birds for flying together against the coming storm. It is their nature, and they cannot help it."

"So how can we?" James Alphaeus said.

"By giving them something better to follow, by giving them someone else to lead," Simon Peter said.

The soldiers scowled.

"The only thing you will be leading any more, you scum, is the way to hell, and your brethren with you," the lead centurion said. "But first, you will lead them all into the arena. Now go!"

With a signal, the soldiers' spears were leveled at the disciples and Barabbas. A servant made his way through their ranks, unlatching their chains, to allow them to fight back in the arena, for greater sport. But in truth, even given their reputations as some of the finest warriors in the land, they were given little chance of survival. They faced daunting odds and a seemingly non-stop array of foes.

It was the evening's climactic event, the ultimate sacrifice, and Herod Antipas was notorious for making this an especially drawn out and bloody affair. He would play with his victims, first unleashing small beasts to wound them, cripple them at most, and then warriors to stalk them and hunt them, to wear them down to nothing, to encircle and cripple them, and then, finally, he would bring on the lions, the tigers, the large beasts, to slaughter them and finish them off in a final orgy of bloodlust.

The disciples' fate would be different, and more spectacular, more drawn out, more dramatic. It would feature a much larger array of warriors and beasts, including strange mutations and demons brought forth to insure their doom. Herod Antipas knew of their reputation, knew of this magnificent array of warriors, and would take no chances on their survival. It was for the sake of his reign, his grip on power, and to set an example, against any others who would dare to risk sedition against the crown, against his crown, or against the authority of Rome, which he ultimately served.

But in all, in truth, what mattered most to him was that it made for good, entertaining sport.

Herod Antipas was, in many ways, like his father, but in many ways nowhere near as cunning, harsh and conniving. Having grown up in royalty and having been pampered since a young age, he had never known battle of his own, unlike his sire, and had instead found blood to be little more than entertainment to him, the loss of life of little consequence or significance other than to his sport and caprice. His enemies would be captured and he would take great pleasure in seeing them killed slowly. Unlike his father, who would brook little tolerance for such things and would act decisively, quickly, brutally, Herod Antipas preferred to play with his victims, to enjoy their deadly denouement.

And so it was with the disciples. Herod Antipas, in truth, bore them little fear or even resentment. He could not have cared less about them. He knew they wanted him dead and overthrown, or at least cowed. He could not have that. Therefore they needed to be destroyed. But he found them to be of such insignificance to his life, of such little danger and consequence directly to him, that their deaths were seen as little more than something to be savored, enjoyed, as any others.

He also saw their deaths as the culmination of something much more, the end of a movement against him that would once more leave him safe, or relatively so, to hopefully live out a life longer than that of his father, and avoiding his father's fate. There were few he feared in this world, and none he had laid eyes upon since his childhood. To him, the disciples were human warriors, no different than his finest guard, and therefore beneath him, beneath his concern.

With a sign from the king, the soldiers pressed the disciples on, out of the dimness of the tunnel and into the harsh light of the early evening and the oppressive humidity of the arena.

Trying to remain steady, trying to retain their faith, they slowly submitted and strode out to meet their fate.

But one remained defiant, one refused to slump his shoulders and his head remained high, a sly look upon his face.

The soldiers took notice and scoffed.

"For a man about to die, run down by warriors and ripped apart by beasts, you seem very confident, Barabbas."

Barabbas smiled.

"I always am."

TWELVE

It was a harsh, desolate space, rock and sand stained with blood and strewn with bone and uneaten detritus of the dead.

Weapons dropped in death throes littered the ground, waiting to be claimed by those doomed to enter the arena's maw in the name of entertainment, sport for those gathered to watch them from the safety of the stands.

The disciples knew full well the rules of the arena. They had avoided it as spectators out of distaste, but word of its torture and spectacle was hard to escape as it provided conversational fodder for the masses, who were both thrilled and cowed by its perversions. Masses kept in line by their darkest fears of finding themselves as sport rather than spectator.

Only Barabbas had been a regular visitor to its caverns. He had traveled in shadow, studied the arena, learning its ways and its secrets, for he knew one such as him would likely one day find himself within its jaws, and his only chance of escape would be through chance or chicanery.

He had been betrayed, captured and sentenced to die, all by design. Manipulated into place by the machinations of the Silent Hand, to insure the sequence of allowing the Christ to die and descend.

And now, Barabbas was once more in place, not by plan, but by fate.

If the disciples were to face this, and overcome it, they would need his knowledge. For while they were of great skill and training, they were not of his ilk in regard to experience in the darker realms of the empire.

They were common men of uncommon character for their times, chosen to be of the people for the people to relate to the people. For common men would relate to common people, and if those men demonstrated amazing fidelity and moral fiber, they provided an accessible example that others could achieve.

They were magnificent warriors, a cadre of hand-picked fighters aligned to protect the Christ and surround him with a stunning lineage of character. But among them were others who would go unsung, unwritten in history's pages, also by design, in order for them, and their order, to remain sub rosa.

Those men like Barabbas.

He had been chosen for this moment. To steal away the disciples. For if he was unsuccessful in releasing them from their imprisonment, as he had been, then he would be the only one who could lead them into the arena, keep them safe, until…

"Go!" the centurions pointed their spears towards the disciples in line, leading them out, through the tunnel, and into the sadistic jaws of the arena, and as they walked with heavy strides out onto the sand of its maw, a great cheer went up through the people, those same people who had cheered for them not so long before, as they had walked with the Christ through this city.

"We have before us, those condemned," the herald called out to the delight of the crowd, as the disciples tentatively looked about, their façade of courage betrayed by the fear in their eyes.

"The disciples of the seditionist and rebel Jesus who called himself the Christ, the Son of God, and who has been tried and executed for his treason this day," the herald continued. "Those condemned to die as his accomplices include the ones called Simon Peter, Jude, Bartholomew, Matthew, Thomas, Philip, Andrew, Simon, James Alphaeus and Barabbas.

"For their crimes as traitors against the Roman Empire they have been condemned to public execution in the claws of the arena, by authority of our Emperor Tiberius, our governor Pontius Pilate and our sitting king, Herod Antipas."

At the announcement of his name, Herod Antipas slowly rose from his richly decorated throne, surrounded in a private box by his guards and Pilate.

The king raised his arms and the crowd cheered, and he lowered them and silence blanketed the arena, as per custom.

The king looked down upon the men in the arena and a sinister smile curled over his face.

"You are hereby sentenced to die, torn apart and devoured by the beasts and warriors of the arena, your flesh left to rot, your bones left to be ground into the dirt as this place of defilement remains your sole resting ground," Herod Antipas said. "Do you wish to beg for mercy? If so, I, and the crowd, will be delighted to hear your pleas."

The disciples shuffled uncomfortably, silent, but one stepped forward.

"You will get no such pleasure from us," Matthew called out. "Our deaths may come, but our lives will outstrip yours, Antipas!"

"Your lives will not outstrip the hour," the king said, as the crowd joined him in laughter.

"I would rather die on my feet," Simon Peter cried, "than live on my knees bowing to scum like you."

"You may die on your knees as well," Herod Antipas said. "We will wager which way you will be slain."

"Herod Antipas, you are little more than a snake, belly, heart and mind to the dirt, your power unearned and undeserved," Simon Peter spat. "But take heed, the time of your elitist scum will soon be through."

"And who will see it to its end? You?"

"Not I, but one much greater than I could ever hope to be."

Herod Antipas sighed, then his lips curved into a devious smile.

"Your king is dead, tortured and defiled, his soul sent in ritual to hell, where Satan awaited him with the open fangs of millions. And you and your fellow dissidents shall soon join him, if not in hell, then at least in death."

Barabbas stepped forward.

And the crowd became strangely charged.

A divisive figure, Barabbas was equally loved and loathed for his reputation and actions. Some saw him as little more than a petty thief and rebel, his actions making the rulers all the more brutal in their desire to stomp out his calls for rebellion and therefore making the lives of the masses all the more miserable. But others saw in Barabbas the freedom and heart of their people. He was well known for his thieving ways,

true, but just as known for his generosity in stealing only from
the rich and the ruling class and using that pilfered wealth to feed
and clothe the poor and finance his attempts at overthrowing the
Romans and the despotic rule that characterized their region. To
some, he was a hero, even if they knew all too well that they
could never show their admiration, at least not in a public forum
where to do so may mean death.

Still, it was less than a day earlier that he had been
brought out in chains before many of them, alongside the Christ,
and when given the choice between which would gain release,
many of those now watching the spectacle had cheered loudly
for Barabbas. So it was a strange sight to see him, again in
chains, despite their calls for his release, and now facing the
certain death of the arena.

"Herod Antipas," Barabbas said. "You laugh, but as
always it is the sick cackle of a coward, one of distance from
battle, the weak whimper of one who allows others to take his
risk while he cowers above the fray. If you were a strong king,
you would face me alone in the arena and prove your mettle by
besting me with your own steel. But you are not. You are a
pathetic weakling who sends other men to do your bidding. You
are a shame to your people and a cheap whore of Rome. We will
never bow to you, but only to the true king whose legend and
legacy will outlive your twisted, petty rule. Your power is an

undeserved fluke of birth and you have done nothing to justify it, or our respect of it. We may die today, but our deaths will be more valiant and worthy in their brevity than your pathetic life will ever be in its longevity.

"Antipas, you are nothing more than a petty thug, a cheap harlot, with nothing but your luck of birth to your credit. You may kill me, but you will never kill that truth, and you will never kill the knowledge in your heart that that is all you are, and all you ever will be."

As Barabbas spoke, a buzz of whispers infected the crowd, as his words seeped into them. And into Herod Antipas, whose face curdled into a sickened grimace.

The king regained himself, flaring with shame and hatred, giving the sign to the gatekeepers of the gladiators and beasts.

"Kill them!" Herod Antipas shouted. "Kill them all!"

THIRTEEN

The crowd stirred, paused for just a moment, then erupted in a growing wave of bloodlust.

Cheap goblets of wine were raised and gulped, sweaty faces leered and laughed. And the masses leaned towards the killing floor for a better look at what was about to transpire.

They watched as the disciples scrambled to grasp weapons from the blood-soaked ground, to arm themselves as the gates began to rise and the first wave of gladiators, clad in spiked armor and bearing nets, demonic looking weapons and spears tipped with white-hot steel, emerged and moved towards the disciples. They advanced upon them, with evil in their eyes and cracked smiles upon their lips, as the lions and beasts held in chains growled in hunger behind them.

The crowd of the arena was now in full frenzy, leering in drunken revelry as the gladiators and beasts crept around and surrounded the doomed disciples, slowly, slowly, as was the custom of the arena, to build suspense.

The masses which not long before had cheered with these men as they entered Jerusalem with the Christ, this crowd which had mere hours before chanted for the release of Barabbas, now yelled themselves hoarse in delight over their impending doom.

All… but three men.

Three men of unusual stature and aura, cloaked in dark robes, who had remained still in the sea of fury and bloodlust.

Three men who exchanged glances as with a rush the centurions tore across the ground, weapons raised, at the circle of undermanned and poorly armed disciples.

But just as quickly, the three robed figures in the crowd joined hands and a power surged through them, as a beam of light burst from them, to the heavens and down as a bolt of lightning that struck the killing grounds and shook the arena, throwing the would-be executioners back and encircling the disciples in a protective ring of fire.

The three doffed their worn, dusty disguises to reveal brilliant armor and ethereal fabrics, the garb of the sacred warriors of S'iam B'ala.

The robes of the Magi.

Three men – the same men who three decades before had emerged from the Glowing City in the East to defend the mother and father of the Christ, who had fought demons and warriors to see to it that Jesus was born within the sacred spires of Bethlehem. Three, ninja wizards of amazing strength and power that the worlds of men had never before seen.

Gaspar, possessed of immense strength and will, unable to be corrupted by the evil of any demon. Thick as an ox, with rippled muscle bulging through his robes, he was possessed of an intimidating pillar of power upon which his gigantic, chiseled head rested. He was a massive trunk of a man, of foreboding presence and deadly girth, with olive skin smooth about a face like granite. His countenance was a severe, brutal beast made bearable only by soft, open eyes wide and expansive as the sky. Like the other two, he was a deadly swordsman and possessed of the arcane crafts, but his greatest potency was his strength, of mind and body, of more than a hundred men.

Melchior, a brilliant wizard and healer and a warrior of unparalleled speed and agility. With a taut, feline air, he had bare wisps of facial hair the color of the rusted skies of autumn carved upon his chin, a shaved head and a round, weathered face the tone of whipped sand and eyes of eerie silver-blue. He was a master of the ancient arts, possessed of countless totems and tokens almost as old as the world itself, and brilliant at the magick of energy, able to heal and kill with the touch of a hand, and manipulate all matter within his auric range, even to the point of opening doors between worlds.

And Balthazar, the most powerful of the three, both a master warrior and a wizard on par with any demon short of Satan himself. Likewise wiry and blade-like in profile as Melchior, Balthazar was the tallest of the three, with skin dark and smooth as a panther, sharp facial hair, a halo of ebony locks and a sleek, regal gait. His smile was generous, wide and inviting and his eyes tremendous and violet, lying like jewels amidst a throne of haltingly high and pronounced cheekbones and an aquiline nose. A cunning swordsman and brilliant scholar of the ancient arts, he was the most powerful wizard to stride the old worlds and into the new, able to travel between dimensions and bearing a majestic light and purity protecting him from the evils and manipulations of the demons within those nether realms, more than any mortal man before him.

In a flush of lightning and a storm of wind they rose from the stands and propelled themselves into the arena, landing on their feet in the midst of the disciples, ready for battle.

Herod Antipas looked upon them, and his blood ran to ice.

He knew well, the legends of these men.

And an unholy fear gripped his soul.

"Release the gates!" he cried. "Release them all!"

Quickly, the rusty portals were yanked upward and a flood of men and beasts, of earthly and supernatural origin, were hurled into the arena, fangs and claws and sharpened steel bared and ready as they surged towards the Magi and disciples.

The three Magi, Balthazar, Gaspar and Melchior, in unison with the most powerful mages of the disciples, Jude, Barabbas and Simon Peter, had positioned themselves to take on the brunt of the attack from the supernatural beasts, with the rest of the disciples handling the human warriors and centurions. Their steel and sorcery clashed mightily against the onslaught, building a growing circle of death about them, as the souls of wicked men and hungry abominations alike were ripped from their bodies, falling at the hands of the holy warriors.

Wave upon wave of new would-be assassins emerged from the pits.

A dervish of weaponry and savagery stormed against the holy warriors. Gladiators, beasts, mutations of demon offspring with spikes of rust jutting from their skulls and teeth sharpened to impale the necks of men. An army of the fierce and depraved.

They flung themselves with fury against the Magi and disciples and into the fangs of their steel, slashing through the hot, humid stench of the arena, the slice of warrior steel and the frigid blue flames of holy magick burning through all opposition.

Herod Antipas and Pilate grew nervous and ragged but the crowd was pitched to a frenzy at the awesome spectacle unfolding before them.

None could emerge victorious against the awesome might of the Magi and disciples, until finally, the arena's dangers were spent, the jaws of death which had claimed so many others were toothless, only an army of corpses, a perverse circle, a wall of death piled high around those who moments before had been condemned and looked doomed to die.

The crowd sat stunned.

They had never seen power of this nature.

Never known it existed.

Never seen such resistance, let alone victory, among the condemned.

Herod Antipas and Pilate were fast to overcome their shock.

"Archers! In position!" Herod Antipas cried. "Destroy them!"

The soldiers positioned about the arena to police the crowd were now tasked to dismiss those within it, and they moved fast to bring their bows to bear upon them. But the Magi were quicker.

Balthazar shouted an ancient incantation, raised his hands as a mist shrouded them, a cage of flame surrounded them, burning the rain of arrows into cinders.

A thick, white smoke rose and whirled with hurricane force about them, whipping about the arena, and in a flash of light all the holy warriors were gone. Disappeared in the fading light of the day, leaving only the guttural fears of the men of power and the new doubts of those subjected to that earthly tyranny, in their wake.

FOURTEEN

Caiaphas led the centurions through the town, the prone figure of James, unconscious, slung between two of the soldiers, caught in a net, and the weeping Mary, mother of Jesus, being guided forward at the point of a sword. The crowds parted with gasps, both in fear and shock.

"Should we not be less forceful or conspicuous, Caiaphas?" the soldier at his side said. "The sight of this could act as a warning, or it could boil the blood and incite the rebellion."

"The rebellion is dead, as these two soon will be," Caiaphas said.

"The only one who will die today is you, Caiaphas!" a voice cried from above.

They looked up, but the dark figure, clad in the warrior's garb of the Silent Hand, was already within their midst, hurtling razor-sharp shuriken into the necks of the soldiers, sending them crumpling to the ground, and dispatching the rest upon the fang of her dual x'ett swords.

The soldiers, once past the surprise of the attack, put up a valiant battle, and steel rattled throughout the harsh afternoon air.

But it was for naught.

Within minutes, their bodies were littered along the ground, all at the feet of the one who had claimed their lives.

She was dark and lithe, with hair pulled back in warrior's way and a severe countenance, a painful beauty, marked with scars. Her eyes blazed with hatred and vengeance as she burned her glance into Caiaphas.

She was the apprentice of Magdalene and the Arimathean.

One of the fiercest warriors of the kingdom.

Tanara the Sin Eater.

Caiaphas moved to grab Mary, to use her as a shield, but Tanara anticipated his cowardice, and sent two gleaming shuriken into his hand and arm, causing him to cry out in pain as they dropped to his side, useless, and he fell away from Mary, who fled to the side of the street where James' body had been dropped.

Caiaphas pulled his sword, but again, Tanara was too fast and her shuriken struck flesh, severing fingers and sending his steel to the ground.

She strode towards him forcefully, and the crowd about them parted in stunned silence.

"I am a man of god!" Caiaphas cried, the sweat of his corpulent form now stained with tears of self-pity and indignation.

"You are nothing of the sort," Tanara scowled, standing over him. "Your power, your influence and your income all rely on convincing the masses that you are their conduit to your god, that you and your priestly brethren are their sole gatekeepers to salvation. The Christ tells his followers you, your church, any church, is irrelevant. He says that God lies within us, around us all, and we need only to believe to belong. He says we need only speak, to ask, to talk to our God ourselves, without any priests, without any help at all. And it costs not one ounce of spilled blood or given gold in sacrifice. His very words, his very existence, makes you, and for that matter all men who claim to be God's gatekeepers, completely irrelevant.

"You are a traitor to your people, your religion and the one true God. Your only masters are Rome and your own depraved wants."

She pulled a glittering golden blade from her belt, one decorated with ancient runes.

Caiaphas recognized it immediately, and his face froze in fear.

It was Arantioch.

"No!" Caiaphas called out.

Arantioch. A soulsblade. A golden weapon crafted by her mentor, the Arimathean, and given to Tanara by him as protection on her quest, to split through any magickal defense offered by a human. Designed to combat the dark craft of men like Caiaphas, on a multi-dimensional level. For not only did it take the life of the one it dispatched, it also captured their soul, their essence, keeping it captive in a desolate limbo until it was cleansed of its evil. It was, like the holy swords of S'iam B'ala, both a weapon and an entity in and of itself, one whose full powers were known to only the Magi.

"Your only god is gold," she said, raising the blade, "and so you shall be taken to death by it."

And she dropped the blade into him with one thrust to the jugular, and he was gone, body and soul, and some measure of revenge had been slaked upon the man who had sold her, as a child, into bondage.

FIFTEEN

Ten years after he had killed Herod and left Jerusalem, the Arimathean returned, this time with the Magi.

After Herod's death and the passing of the Time of the Dragon, its end marking that the infant Christ was again immune to danger, as written in the prophecies, the boy and his family were accompanied from Egypt back to their homeland. Now safe, at least for the next three decades, Jesus was raised with his mother and father, as a carpenter's son.

However, while humble, he was forever tied to his destiny.

And so, as he reached adolescence, the Magi and Arimathean arrived, to secret the Christ away once more to the East, for various travels known only to the few men of God privy to the secret ways.

However, when the three Magi left with the Christ, the Arimathean remained behind for a short time, to secure protection for Jesus' parents and to attend to various errands to prepare the way for Christ's eventual return.

At the time, there was a rift beginning within the Sanhedrin, the ancient religious men of the land. The old guard had begun dying off, some would say with help from the Roman hierarchy, and a new guard began taking over. But along with them came a few to their midst who had been secretly helped into place by the Romans, who sought more subtle control over the lands which had long been simmering in rebellion to Roman rule. Eventually, they would be counterbalanced by good men, and those put in place by the secret sect the Silent Hand, including the noble Nicodemus and the Arimathean, who would call himself Josephus, in honor of the father of the Christ. But for a few murky years, the transition was dire.

These hollow men of rule were little more than puppets for the Empire, mouthing the right words and following the holy ways with great pomp and circumstance, but more often than not merely taking advantage of situations when needed, when they arose. They had little feeling or commitment to anything but their greed for power and lust for the gold which crossed their palms in exchange for complicity and subtle influence exerted when Rome ordered them to do so.

Among these hollow men was one of particularly virulent hypocrisy and appetites.

A man named Caiaphas.

Abusing the laws and old ways, he built his fortune through the sale of the promise of heaven, or at least the absolution of sin, usually at the expense of the poor, suffering, women and children. Among his more abhorrent practices was the selling of females of all ages, including those used as "sin eaters," women who would be held captive in villages and tortured, often having small wooden or steel spikes stabbed into them and embedded in their flesh, with each representing a sin the torturer would want absolved. It was believed that by doing so, the slave would absorb the sin which was symbolized, and thought to be carried by, the spike.

When the Arimathean heard of this practice, he used every channel for knowledge to find the camps and villages where the sin eaters were housed, in order to free them. For some, it was too late, and the bodies found by him caused his eyes to fill with tears and his chest to fill with rage.

As for those alive, some were easily pried from their captivity with a few persuasive words or coins exchanged.

Others required more insistent techniques.

And so it was for one particular girl, of an unknown number of years.

He found her in a cage, barely clothed, near death and starvation, beaten and broken, her body riddled with the scars and slivers of wood and steel embedded by her captors, who refused to free her, until their tongues could refuse no more, silent in their mouths, albeit for those gagging in their death throes.

The Arimathean strode over their bodies, dispassionate, reserving any pity for the girl they had held captive, in a shoddy, jagged cage, over which held a sign with one word, "unclean."

She breathed heavy and ragged, shrieking and sorry, as he broke her cage open and offered his hand to her. She did not know him. She only knew what she had just seen. Death at his hands. Death with such violence and speed that even she had never seen before.

And so, he waited.

He left her food, water and clothing, and waited for her to emerge from her cage.

For three days, despite the door remaining open, despite the Arimathean's slumber under the moon, despite his distance during the sunlight, she remained in the cage.

Until finally, on the third day, she slowly, tentatively emerged, hovering at the door of the cage and barely nudging it open.

The Arimathean watched as she pushed it aside, scampered out, began to run, then fell, in pain.

He walked over to her.

"I will not hurt you," he said. "I have come to save you. I have stayed to protect you, to watch over you."

She looked at him, uncertain, shaking.

"I understand you have little reason to trust anyone," he said. "But you have seen what I have done to your captors, to free you, to protect you. You need not fear."

She looked about at the bodies of the men who had tortured her. Looked at the food and water the Arimathean had given her, the clothing upon her from him. She looked into his eyes, the color of the horizon at dusk, burned sienna and flickering gold. She saw his pain. His suffering. His faith.

And so she raised her arm, outstretched her hand, and let him pull her up, until she leapt to him, holding him tight and exhausting her tears and sobs against him, for what seemed like ages, years of pain being released. And then she sat, drained, next to him, and she ate and drank, voraciously, until she finally felt, for the first time, at rest.

"What is your name, child?" the Arimathean said.

"I...I can't remember," the girl said, softly.

"Do you have a family?"

"They are...all dead."

She wept.

"I have nowhere to go," she said. "I have nothing. I have no home."

The Arimathean took her into his arms, pulled off his cloak and covered her shivering body.

"Yes you do," he said. "And I will take you there."

She began to sob, and pulled herself close to him.

"Thank you," she said. "Thank you."

He held her and let her extinguish her tears against him.

"You are safe now," he said. "You are safe."

"But I am nothing," she cried, "I am nothing. I am nameless and wasted, only called unclean by the men who kept me."

He wiped away the girl's tears. Looked into her eyes.

"Where I come from, there is a mountain range," he said. "It is jagged and forbidding, and difficult to cross.

"When it is decided it is time for a child to travel into adulthood, boy or girl, to become a man or woman, they will be trained and prepared and will be sent out to cross those mountains, to collect a rare flower that grows only in their mists, and then return it to our land.

"I often trekked through those jagged paths in returning to my home, for while they could be cold and forbidding, they could also be pure and beautiful.

"And in the dawn's break, when the light passes over their clawed peaks and they explode in color, the stones a crystal canvas, they are breathtaking, striking, and there is no place more magical in this world.

"Those mountains," he said, "our people call them Tanara."

She looked down, then up at him.

"Tanara," she said.

He smiled at her.

His lips curved in a soft smile, calm and reassuring, and he put his arms around her, keeping her warm.

"That, my child," he said. "That is your name."

SIXTEEN

Wine, heat, anger and shame reddened the faces of
Herod Antipas and Pilate as they strode through the courtyard to
the palace.

"You fear for your life, because a band of rebels foments
dissent, but you should not," Pilate said. "This is an
inconvenience, but not one that cannot be overcome. The streets
are packed with zealots and every season brings a new so-called
messiah, and all meet the same end, the same death, while we
live on to watch their demise."

"You fear for your life as well, Pilate," Herod Antipas
said. "And you should be fearing for your life if this movement
is allowed to take hold. I have seen such zealotry on the rise
throughout my reign, seemingly led by a new messiah every
week, a ranting dirty rebel on every corner shouting for heaven
to strike us down. But none have been the Christ. None have
brought forth the return of the Magi."

"The Magi are a complication, but not one that cannot be controlled as well," Pilate said.

"The Christ has been slain in ritual, his soul sent to hell, his body sold to the depraved, who will defile it as they will. Tomorrow morning it will be dragged through the streets and returned to its death place. And his followers will soon be in chains again, folly for our entertainments."

"I suppose I should share your confidence, Pilate," Herod Antipas said. "But for some reason, my gut is uneasy, I have a bad feeling about this. There are no men I fear on this world. None but the Magi. And you know very well my reasons for fearing them, you know well of their power."

"You were merely taken aback by the emergence of the Magi," Pilate said. "And rightfully so, for, yes, we are both well aware of their power. But it is not infinite, and they too can be slain by the demons we will bring forth to this world."

"This is true," Herod Antipas said, his mood lifting slightly.

"They could not have gotten far, we will send out an army to scour Jerusalem for them!" Pilate said. "I will have Judas lead the elite. They will not escape!"

"We must do so immediately," Herod Antipas said. "We cannot allow them to hide for long. We must make sure the body of the Christ is secure. We cannot allow them to abscond with it."

"There is no worry in that regard," Pilate said. "As I said, I have taken care of it. The soldiers have given the body to the Sodomites who will return it to Golgotha at midday tomorrow. Then, a Sanhedrin will claim it and seal it away in a stone tomb, where it will be guarded by our elite."

"A Sanhedrin?" Herod Antipas said. "Can he be trusted? My spies have heard of infiltration of the Sanhedrin by the Silent Hand."

"He came in the name of Caiaphas," Pilate said. "Caiaphas will not betray us. He is too drunk on power to allow it to be taken from him."

"Yes," Herod Antipas said. "And it is best for the body to be entombed as one of his own people in a sacred space, for appearance's sake alone, to quell any potential uprising."

"And while the people are led to believe this is an honor of their beliefs," Pilate said, "that tomb may as well be a prison, for how many guards will surround it, at least until the third day."

Herod Antipas smiled.

"Excellent," Herod Antipas said. "Caiaphas has served us well. He has delivered the body, he will soon deliver the mother of the Christ, and we will have all we need to create our army. Caiaphas will not betray us."

They entered the palace and as they did, a strange, oblong object came tumbling towards them, sickeningly thumping across the floor before landing in a disgusting mess on the marble inches from their feet.

Glassy, deadened eyes stared up at them, piercing above a gaping mouth and a face now perpetually frozen in a grimace.

A human head.

The head of Caiaphas, the Sanhedrin.

"Well, congratulations on finally being correct about one thing," said a figure sitting upon the throne of Herod Antipas. "Caiaphas will betray no one any longer."

The figure rose and descended from the throne, and as he did, the array of brilliantly garbed and armored soldiers arranged about him stood at attention, in formation.

"That… thing was thrown at our regiment as we passed on our way here," the figure said. "Thrown by a man who was quickly relieved of the arm which bent it our way, and relieved of his misbegotten life, along with the other rebellious miscreants who dared to try to impede us.

"However, I find it unseemly that your people behave in such a way," the figure said, "especially towards one so clearly their superior."

Pilate froze with fear and then quickly bowed on one knee.

"I wish I could say it was a pleasure to meet you, but it is not," the scowling figure said as he approached Herod Antipas, pointing a thick finger to the ground before the king. "Bow before me. Bow, before your emperor, Tiberius."

SEVENTEEN

The disciples rendezvoused at the tomb of Christ, joined
by the three Magi, the Arimathean, Magdalene and Tanara.
James had fully recovered, administered to by Tanara's healing
potions, and he accompanied them, with Mary, for her safety.

"How did you know?" Barabbas said, to the Magi.

"You did not meet us at the rendezvous point, we made
quick inquiries and there was a buzz being sent out among the
populace about a new, special attraction in the arena this
evening," Gaspar said. "It seems we were correct in assuming
the worst."

"Are you not always correct in assuming that?"
Barabbas said.

"Not always," Balthazar said. "Otherwise, you would
not be alive."

In addition to their gratitude for saving them from the
hell of the arena, the disciples were somewhat in awe of the
Magi. They had heard tales of them, certainly, and some of them

– Simon Peter, Jude, Matthew -- had met them or trained with them, but for the most part they were warriors of legend, almost myth, and seeing them in person was surreal.

"I have often heard tales of them, but this is my first experience with the Magi," Bartholomew said.

"I as well," Thomas said. "I have heard many different tales, that they are mighty wizards and kings from the East, that they are archangels, that they are the watchers or Elohim from the old scriptures, immortal beings who once visited the earth on chariots of gold."

"You know of them best, Simon Peter, who are they?" James Alphaeus said.

"Those legends, that they are kings, or archangels, are all what they would have you believe," Simon Peter said. "Those chosen as Magi are of both worlds – half-human, half-Elohim. Few, not I, know how they are conceived or selected, but they are possessed of immense power and glory beyond even the greatest of mortal men. It is true that some scribes have written of them as archangels, or soldiers of God, but in truth, perhaps not even they know the full extent of their origins, or their power."

"Is the Arimathean, too, one of their order?" James Alphaeus said.

Simon Peter looked over at the Arimathean, then back to the disciples.

"Fewer still know of his past, his power, or his allegiance," Simon Peter said. "He travels with the Magi, and I have heard he was at least once of their order, but he is a man who follows no path but his own."

The disciples were silent a moment, contemplating the warriors before them.

"Whatever their origins, we, we are happy and blessed that they use their power for good, for the good of humanity," Simon Peter said.

"Do all? Have they all used that power for good?" Thomas said.

"Most... almost all," Simon Peter said. "But not all."

The Arimathean called them all to attention as they gathered around him and the other Magi.

Before them were an array of horses and three carts, each containing a body, wrapped tightly in linens.

"The Christ's soul has descended to purgatory and the rings of hell to open the gates for those deserving," Balthazar said. "But that leaves his body vulnerable until Sunday sunrise. It is a hollow shell, still imbued with the potential for the power he would wield upon this plane. If another soul or demon would inhabit it, they too could use that power, for unfettered destruction and evil. It would turn the Christ's body into little more than a puppet, turned into the Antichrist by its demon inhabitant."

"But what demon would have the power to…" Jude said.

"Satan," Melchior said.

"But how?" Bartholomew said.

"Satan has been summoned to this dimensional plane, once more, by Herod Antipas and the forces of Rome," Balthazar said. "They were ready, they had prepared the ritual for his summoning, and at the moment the gates of hell were opened by the Christ's death, Satan himself came stabbing through."

"How can he remain?" Thomas said. "Does he not need a host?"

"They have provided him with several potential hosts, several human bodies to inhabit," Balthazar said, "and will continue to do so, until he can either inhabit the Christ or he is driven back to hell and chained there, unable to leap between the dimensional planes."

"How could that happen? How could God allow such a thing?" Thomas said.

"While he is here, it is enabling the Christ to complete his own quest in the netherworld without Satan's interference," Melchior said. "And remember, God has also brought us together to prevent it from happening."

"We must make haste," Balthazar said. "The forces of evil will waste no time in arraying against us and will take every step to destroy us."

And so, as the day was overcome by night, they set out in three groups, to confuse the enemy.

They would head into the desert, which offered refuge, in more ways than one. From a magickal standpoint, the desert had always been ideal, a blank canvas upon which nature could be employed to full advantage as a weapon when needed. And from a practical standpoint, there were few places to hide in the expanse of sand, dirt and rock. If an attack was coming, they would see it, and be able to gird themselves in preparation.

Each of the three groups fled, taking divergent paths to a rendezvous point they believed offered the greatest spiritual protection.

Bethlehem.

The city where it had all begun, thirty-three years ago, where the infant Christ had been born, and where the core of these warriors had battled evil together to allow his birth to take place.

Bethlehem.

Where ancient ley lines of energy circling and crossing the earth created a sacred spire of protection upon the rise of the Christ.

Bethlehem.

The location to which they knew their opposition would follow, trying to hunt them down and abscond with the body of Christ.

Their plans were clear.

Each of the three groups traveled with a horse, pulling with them a cart and a body, cloaked and tightly wrapped so as to obscure its identity, and wearing holy amethyst to occlude any sorcerous means of identifying it from a distance as the body of the Christ. Therefore, the enemy would have to attack each group individually, to ascertain whether it had the body. And so the enemy would divide its energies, making the pilgrims more difficult to attack, and helping them succeed in their quest. While ostensibly the disciples would be exposed, their destination known, by dividing up into three groups their enemies would be diluted.

None of the groups knew if they were protecting the body of the Christ or not, for reasons of cloaking, for if a demon powerful enough to read the mind of any of them were to do so and found out the true location of the Christ, then they would be able to amass their full forces at that place. Only Balthazar, the most powerful of the Magi, whose mind was impenetrable to even the rankest of demons, was aware of the totality of the plan as well as the true location of the body.

Each group was led by one of the Magi, and therefore was under the protection of the most powerful ninja wizards to walk the worlds of men. Each group was divided and sorted to provide it a variety of strengths.

Gaspar would be accompanied by Magdalene, Bartholomew, James Alphaeus, Jude and Thomas.

Melchior would travel with Simon Peter, Andrew, Tanara and Philip.

Balthazar, with the Arimathean, Simon the Zealot, Matthew and Barabbas, would take the final route.

Keeping an eye over all three groups and thereby maintaining communication between them were the familiars. Messenger birds. White owls. That each of the Magi, Magdalene, Tanara and the Arimathean could use, leaping into the avian's consciousness through mystical means in order to ascertain the movements of each group. To do so for any length of time was a risky maneuver, for it meant sending a brief shard of one's consciousness into the body of another, but it was a necessity.

Each of the birds had been ancient familiars to the Magi, bred in the halls of S'iam B'ala. Seraphim, flying high above Balthazar, had accompanied the warriors and been of service during the first mission of the Christ over three decades earlier. Cherubim, accompanying Melchior, and Electrum, with Gaspar, were untested in such rigorous circumstance, but were trusted companions considered well worthy of the task.

Once prepared, they bid their goodbyes and blessings to one another, each keeping a brave face, but holding within the prayer that this would not be a final farewell.

And then, as the sky grew heavy in indigo and gold, they set out, into the bones of the night and the blood of their destiny.

EIGHTEEN

The man rampaged through the fields sweat-stained and bleeding, a wounded animal, voices swarming through his brain, poisoned by a maniacal laugh.

He thought he heard legions behind him, hunting him down. He could not see them, only thought he could hear them gaining, behind him. He knew that his betrayal was payable only in blood and vengeance, a revenge they, in their blinding anger over the death of one so beloved, they now sought to attain.

It was not like him to feel this fear, to feel so helpless, so weak.

But he did.

He felt drained, feverish, frantic, plagued by the voices of doubt and evil relentlessly stabbing through his skull.

His body tired, his muscles burned, but he kept on, pushing, until, suddenly, he imagined he heard the sounds of battle behind him, the quick clashes of steel and cries of pain and then, he heard nothing more.

Silence.

He kept pushing on.

But still, he heard nothing.

No one pursuing him.

He stopped for a moment, looked around him, looked to
the heavens and began to cry, cry as his eyes burned and his
body shook, and he broke down and fell to the dirt, the dust
clinging to his wet skin and turning his tears into an ebon mask
upon his face.

His mind could not escape his betrayal. It surrounded
him as an ocean and his heart drowned in it.

He pulled out the bag, the deep violet velvet pouch,
heavy with silver pieces. He looked at its ornate sigils painted
upon its side, opened it up and felt the coins warm to his touch,
felt strange sparks as they emanated from the metal onto his
grasp, into his skin, pouring through his flesh, as he felt a strange
web weaving around him, and heard the voices again, low at
first, in harsh whispers like the beginning scratches of cicadas in
the late summer night, then growing louder and louder until they
drowned his head in diabolical, guttural demands.

He felt his hand grasp the silver once more, but it was as
if he was not in control of it.

It was as if he was not in control of his body at all.

Or his mind.

Or heart.

Or soul.

He grabbed the satchel of coins, ran to the edge of a cliff, to a ragged tree, hooked over its edge like a massive claw into the sky over its rocky bed.

He felt his body jerk in motion, tried to stop it, but could not, could feel the rush of flame, cold and dark, within him.

His hands dropped the silver coins in occult patterns about the tree.

He pulled the rope from around his waist.

Hooked it tightly over a slumping branch hanging out over the drop.

He cried and desperately attempted to stop his own hands from hastening the chariot of his demise, but he could not. It was as if they were being controlled by something else, some other entity within him.

And the voices grew louder, louder, in his head.

He felt as the other side of the rope was tied tight, burning around the flesh of his neck.

He heard a deepening cackle in his ear, felt a black hand close around his heart.

And with his last sentient thought a prayer of sorrow and repentance, crying for forgiveness, he felt the demon within him douse that final flame of humanity, take over his body and soul, and hurtle his flesh over the chasm as his neck remained lashed to the tree.

In a quick jerk, his neck was broken, and it was done.

His mortal body was nothing but an empty vessel now.

Waiting to be taken and filled.

And with a loud crack, the branch broke, and the body fell, fell to the ground below, beaten and tattered along the way as it ripped and bounced over the jagged rocks down into the pit.

It crashed and laid motionless for just a moment.

Blood puddled along the ground.

And then, the body began to rise.

Rise.

Rise again.

No longer the man, the human being, it once was.

No longer anything but the image of Judas Iscariot.

Now nothing but a shell, a vessel, a body perfectly possessed.

The new throne of Satan on earth.

NINETEEN

It did not take Tiberius long to seize control of the temple… and the rituals taking place within.

And as the blood and screams flowed with greater urgency, the emperor looked scornfully upon Pilate and Herod Antipas, who had filled themselves with wine and slumped in stupor.

"Rome has taken an interest in this Christ," Tiberius said. "We will be taking over the situation."

He was sharp and regal, with a severe bearing, greying hair cut short upon his head and a face hard and carved in evil. He had the bearing of a man not only completely comfortable with power, but one conniving enough to always be in control of it, and those around him, regardless of their understanding of his will.

Tiberius, as with all emperors, believed himself to be descended from the gods, divine on earth and impervious to human feelings and ways. Like all of his kind, he had been

trained in the mystery schools and knew well the ways of battle
and the dark arts of magick. As the ruler of Rome he was given a
power beyond that of most men.

But the Christ and his followers were beyond him, and
he knew this.

They showed little concern for his rule and authority,
and even his demonic power, fully unleashed, was no match for
the power he had heard displayed by the Christ.

But if that power could be turned, could be manipulated
and used by him in some way, he could rule with even greater
finality.

Tiberius had had a long and fruitful reign, but like all
rulers, he could feel himself in the autumn of his years, and as
such, he watched as the buzzards began to fly about him.
Opportunists, potential emperors, those looking to position
themselves in their favor and those merely licking their teeth at
the prospect of his downfall. He knew even under the best of
circumstances, he would not be long on the throne, and under the
worst he could find himself overthrown before year's end,
drained of life in the night, or stabbed in the back by any number
of potential conspirators.

But if he could harness the power of the Christ, not only
would he be able to crush every viper circling about him, but he
could assume the throne for decades, if not centuries, to come.

His seers had pored over the ancient prophecies and
testaments, discovered the time tables for the Christ's body to be
turned, to be changed into little more than a zombie under his
authority, a weapon, an antichrist, and so he wasted little time in
arriving once he had gotten their news.

"There is no need for worry, Tiberius," Pilate said. "The
situation will soon be well in hand."

"Indeed it will," Tiberius said. "In my hand, it will."

"But you have just arrived," Herod Antipas said. "Do
you have any idea of what...?"

"I have every idea," Tiberius shot back. "I know all."

He paced with them through the palace, past the
entranceway and the initial throne room, into the bowels of the
palace, and the main throne room, still humming with devious
activity, the piles of dead growing as the sorcerous gateway
pulsed above them.

"As you saw when you arrived," Pilate said, "we are
well in control and well on our way to turning the Christ."

"Are you, then?" Tiberius said with a condescending
snort. "Are you, Antipas?"

Tiberius slanted a jagged look at Herod Antipas as the
king averted his eyes from the withering glare of the emperor.

"You know nothing," the emperor said. "You are drunk on power, among other things. You have no idea of the forces you are attempting to harness."

"You are a fool and an idiot, Antipas," Tiberius said through gritted teeth. "You are a child playing with a sword. Your father would throttle you in your cradle if he could know of your monumental stupidity and incompetence."

Herod Antipas looked to Pilate to intervene, but Pilate was chastened, weak, staring down at the ground like a punished boy, and so Herod Antipas summoned the words that had so recently soothed him.

"Tiberius," Herod Antipas said, trying to gain his composure, "why do you fear? The Christ is dead, slaughtered, his body entombed. His followers are scattered rats, easily caught again, and thrown into the arena once more to die for our amusement. And that amusement shall be even greater as they will be sent to die with their would-be saviors, who will provide even greater sport in their deaths! The disciples and even the Magi will not last very long against the new beasts of the arena we are preparing. A few minutes at most. These new warriors should provide for a much grander battle. My vizier…"

Tiberius smiled.

"Your vizier?" Tiberius stretched his arms out. "Where is he?"

"I…I…" Herod Antipas looked about the temple. "I do not know."

"I do," Tiberius said.

Tiberius nodded towards the pit of blood sacrifice, outstretched his arm toward it, and smiled.

"Do you know how much sacrificial energy a vizier holds?" Tiberius said. "Their deaths are quite a bounty."

Herod Antipas winced in hatred and anger.

"A true sorcerous leader does not need a vizier," Tiberius scowled. "A Roman Emperor needs only himself."

Tiberius walked to a servant and grabbed a chalice of wine, took a drink, clenched his teeth, and threw the container across the room, smashing it against the wall.

"You fools!" Tiberius said. "Those were no mere warriors of the Silent Hand, in Judea born! Those were Magi, Watchers from the Golden City! You, Herod Antipas, above all should be aware of their power. Or did you listen to your father not at all? And if the Magi have come, they have come for one reason, to wrest the body of the Christ from us!"

"Tiberius, I assure you, our centurions…" Pilate said. "We have sent them to the tomb, to encircle and secure…"

"Our centurions are nothing against the power of the Magi!"

"But, but, Tiberius, the demons we will bring forth…" Antipas began.

"Would be nothing to the Magi, who defeated those brought forth by your father, who was ten times the mage you are," Tiberius said to Herod Antipas.

Herod Antipas brooded, but Tiberius merely ignored him, until something stunned him to attention.

"Wait!" Tiberius raised his finger angrily to Pilate. "What tomb? I instructed you to bring the Christ's body here to the palace!"

"We were waiting for your arrival, to take it from the tomb to bring here," Pilate said. "We did not want to risk any more unrest, so we allowed it to be placed in the tomb of a Sanhedrin, and summarily surrounded by guards, Roman centurions of the finest…"

Tiberius shook his head violently.

"Sometimes opposition is fomented to create support," Tiberius said. "If one can fire up sufficient antagonism from one side, the other will instantly come to the defense by instinct, often without thinking about what they are actually fighting for, only relishing the battle against their frequent foe. Thus, you can control both sides of the battle."

"What do you mean?" Herod Antipas said.

"I mean that sometimes it is advantageous for your enemies to be enemies with one another," Tiberius said. "If the Christ's followers and the Sanhedrin are meant to oppose each other, they cannot unite against us."

Tiberius shook his head. "You would not understand," he said. "But where is this tomb? Where can we claim the body? And who is this Sanhedrin you speak of?"

"A nobleman of their order, who came with the seal of Caiaphas himself," Pilate said. "A man named Josephus, an Arimathean…"

Tiberius simmered in a fit of anger, casting quickly around the room to a soldier in the corner.

"You," he said to the Judean soldier, in a deceptively calm voice. "Come here."

The soldier ran to Tiberius's side.

"Give me your sword!"

The soldier bowed and handed the weapon to Tiberius, and in one swift and brutal thrust, the Roman jammed it hard into the chest of the stunned man, who spat and gurgled and fell, dead, to the floor.

Antipas and Pilate gasped.

Tiberius pulled the sword out, clenched it in his fist, tightly, and then, with a deep breath, relaxed and let his arm fall to his side.

He let out a deep breath.

Then another.

And another.

And then, he smirked, and turned to face the two men, slowly pacing between and around them.

"Tiberius, my lord, you must forgive us, we did not..." Pilate began, before being silenced by Tiberius's raised hand.

Tiberius sighed as he circled about Antipas.

"Herod Antipas, you amuse me," he purred. "But not enough."

With a quick thrust of his blade, Tiberius ripped through Herod Antipas' chest, stunning him and causing him to drop his chalice to the ground in a violent crash of wine and blood.

"How dare you!" the Judean king cried out, but any other words were lost.

Tiberius pulled him close and whispered into his ear. "You pathetic fool," the Emperor said. "You thought you could harness the antichrist to take over Rome, to overthrow me, and to sit upon the world's throne, to wear its crown? And you thought you could do it without my knowledge? Look upon Pilate, for he is your betrayer, and let that be your last knowledge of this world, that you can trust no one, and your folly is your death. This is the only Roman metal you deserve."

With another rush of steel, Tiberius squeezed the last life from the king, his crown falling from his limp head and onto the gore-splattered marble floor, soon followed by his lifeless body.

Tiberius stood over the corpse for a moment, then sighed, looking back at Pilate.

"It is never as much fun as you think it is going to be," Tiberius said.

He then pointed the sword at Pilate, watched as the governor heaved and sweated and pleaded.

"Tiberius, please, I have been loyal to you, I have been loyal, I told you of his plot and kept you informed all along the way," Pilate said, as he fell to his knees, his hands clutched together, begging for his life.

Tiberius raised the sword, then stilled it, pulled it back to his side, and smirked at the whimpering Pilate.

"Rest assured, Pilate," Tiberius hissed. "You are safe, for now. You have served me well as a spy on this scum, and for that you live, but do not fail me again."

"I will not, emperor, I swear to you, I swear," Pilate said.

"Rise, and throw that fool's body into the flames with the rest of the sacrifices," Tiberius said. "I worry not. Even though our plan will have to be altered slightly, all soon shall fall into place."

Tiberius motioned to two soldiers, who brought him a large, glimmering golden brown egg, sitting upon a red velvet pillow laced with gold.

Tiberius looked into the pit of sacrificial blood welled up before him, at the hellmouth glowing green and putrid at the ceiling of the palace, dipped his sword into the pool and traced a red sigil of blood along the outside of the egg.

The sigil began to glow with a strange crimson light, then mist ochre, and then the egg opened, to reveal a small, hideous creature, looking like a large flea with bat-like wings, in a viscous pool of dark sludge.

"Oh my," Tiberius said, reaching his hand in and petting the flea creature as it emitted a hideous purr, "how much fun we will have with you."

He looked into the crystal ring on his finger, silver, identical to Pilate's.

"Do not worry, Pilate," Tiberius said, gazing admiringly upon the flea-like creature. "I have everything under control."

But then, an explosion rocked the entranceway to the palace, a tremendous wall of flame appeared, and then dissipated, and then, through the black haze, a figure appeared, skin scarred and charred, eyes alight in unholy fire.

Even through the darkness, even through the mangling of its flesh, Pilate instantly recognized the face, instantly knew.

The body and visage of Judas Iscariot.

Now inhabited fully by Satan.

"No, Tiberius," the Judas-Satan symbiote growled. "I am in control here."

TWENTY

The night fell on the Friday the Christ died, and a blood moon rose. Darkness wrapped around the weary travelers, and those in Balthazar's camp were gathered about a small fire. Matthew, Barabbas and Simon the Zealot slept. Balthazar and the Arimathean, long accustomed to little or no sleep, kept watch.

"Two nights, my friend," Balthazar said. "Less than we had to sustain when we first gathered to protect him, before he was born into this world. And we are a far more powerful cadre of warriors joined together at this time."

"But the stakes are even higher," the Arimathean said. "You know as well as I what the prophecies dictate. Their last failure, they knew they had a window to kill him just two years later, and another now, thirty-one years beyond that. But these nights are their last chance, for the next two-thousand years. They know this. They will stop at nothing."

"They will be stopped, by us, by God, who has brought us all together at this time," Balthazar said.

"Perhaps you are right," the Arimathean said. "It is two nights, we are far more than we were three decades past, and Herod Antipas and his chain of viziers are nothing but shadows of his father and his mages."

"Let us not be too confident, however," Balthazar said, laughing.

"I was trying to show you some faith," the Arimathean said. "I thought you would be impressed with my effort."

"Indeed," Balthazar said. "Very impressive."

The two laughed, slightly.

"You are right to believe," Balthazar said. "Hope is the most precious currency there is."

"If we do succeed, though, who will be here two millennia from now, to protect him, when he returns?" the Arimathean said.

"Always the pessimist," Balthazar said.

"Always the pragmatist," the Arimathean said.

"In time, my friend, in time," Balthazar said. "First, we survive this mission."

The two smiled, and looked off into the night, silently, and Balthazar glanced, sideways, towards his friend.

In the past few years, he had felt something. Something that perhaps explained the question. Something that perhaps the Arimathean himself had dared to consider.

Something he had long suspected, about the Arimathean.

Something that could not merely be explained by his extended time in S'iam B'ala with the other three Magi.

He had aged seemingly not at all in the past thirty-three years, going back to before his time in the Glowing City, where mortal years slow to a crawl and time travels far slower, giving those between worlds such as the Magi amazing restorative powers and the ability to slow the aging process to a crawl.

No, this was beyond that.

Going back to the years before his time in the Glowing City.

Going back to the last time the Magi had been on a mission of this sort.

Back to when the Arimathean had been at the door of death, and even partially beyond it, and to drag him back into the living, Balthazar had dared to go with him to the space between worlds, the nether realms, where time warps, the dimensions blur and all manner of creatures good and evil beyond the imaginations of man wander and feed.

For decades, to this day, they had never spoken of what they saw and experienced in those realms.

But neither forgot.

And neither, once they had returned to earth, had aged more than a moment beyond that day.

The two other Magi, as expected, had aged little, given their superhuman constitution, but still, there were some subtle signs. And the humans they had encountered those three decades ago – Simon Peter, Magdalene and Jude, all children at the time, and the Revelator, then a younger man -- had grown to adulthood and beyond.

But there was no marking of age, no passing of time, between him and the Arimathean.

And so Balthazar wondered.

About the question asked.

And the questions yet to be.

But they were questions for another time.

The task at hand was arduous enough.

Their familiars had given them enough information for them to know that Herod Antipas was steeping his temple in ritual, amassing the dark arts, hoping to transform the body of the Christ. Now he would be focusing that sinister energy upon them, attempting to steal the body back, and he would care little how many, if not all of them, were killed in the process.

The owls remained above the three groups, connecting them all, and for a moment, Balthazar blinked into his familiar, seeing his fellow two Magi and their companions, safe.

For now.

But not for long, he knew.

And so they remained on watch.

Waiting.

For the first inevitable attack.

TWENTY-ONE

It was a clear night, deceptively calm, with the slightest chill, and so Gaspar's camp had built a fire.

Bartholomew, James Alphaeus, Thomas and Jude had spent most of the evening squabbling over their journey and its elements, but had finally fallen asleep, while Gaspar and Magdalene remained awake, alert.

"I am not sure which will bring me greater pain, the demons we will face or these four and their constant arguing with one another," Gaspar said.

Magdalene smiled. "They are contrary men and certainly unafraid to share their opinions," she said.

"Which is good, it is good to test the mind as well as the body," Gaspar said, "although with this lot it is a never-ending exercise."

"True," Magdalene said. "Although this is one reason why the Christ assembled us as his disciples. He not only needed warriors, people of great strength, he wanted those who were of great mind and word as well, to eventually spread the word of his following."

"To men, and to women," Gaspar said, with a smile.

"To both, yes," Magdalene said, smiling in return. "That is one of the many reasons I have devoted myself to him, to his following. He sees us all as equal. He sees us all the same. As people, as creatures of God, deserving of love and respect."

"Much as the Magi and the Silent Hand," Gaspar said.

"I am, my life is, evidence of that," Magdalene said.

Gaspar smiled, nodded.

There was a pause, as both looked to the sky, listened to the sounds of the night, the fire crackling gently.

"What is it like," Magdalene said, "to be a Magi? How did you… were you a… orphan like me?"

"Yes," Gaspar said. "In a way. Melchior and Balthazar, all three of us, we were descendants of Magi, of those raised to walk between worlds. But their parents, they, survived long into their lives, they raised them, trained them, and lived long before passing. Mine… did not. My father was a mighty warrior, he, died in a quest much like this one. But when he did, he died with honor and, I believe, with happiness, knowing he would join her, my mother."

Gaspar looked down, picked up a handful of sand, let it fall through his fingers.

"She... died in childbirth," he said. "She died having me. I... never met her."

"I am sorry," Magdalene said.

"Thank you," Gaspar said. "I... someday... I will meet her... see them both again. In the afterlife. In the ethereal spires of the Golden City, in the heavens above this world."

"Yes," Magdalene said, with a gentle smile. "I am certain you will."

Gaspar went silent, and the two remained without words for a long while.

"You are a creature of the night," Gaspar said, "like your mentor."

"Which mentor? The Revelator or the Arimathean?"

"Both," Gaspar said, with a slight laugh.

"Both have been very important to me, in different ways," Magdalene said.

"In different ways, indeed, one more a father and the other... a friend," Gaspar said, raising an eyebrow. "But both are men of great prominence and little sleep."

"Indeed," she said, raising an eyebrow in return.

A pregnant silence blossomed between them.

"How long do you think this peace will last?" she said.

"As long as they are asleep," Gaspar said, nodding to the disciples.

Magdalene laughed. "If only that were our only worry on this trek," she said.

Gaspar's face grew serious.

"I can only guess," he said. "The attacks will not be constant. They will likely be massive, imposing, involving major arcana demons or armies of minor arcana. Herod Antipas, like his father, lacks much subtlety in the way of the dark arts, so he will likely deluge us with a garish display of power. And demons such as that require much energy and preparation to summon, so, given it has not been long since we have escaped and therefore they have had little time to prepare, we should not see the first attack for a while, perhaps not until daybreak. If we survive that one, there probably will not be another attack for at least half a day, and, again, after that, the same. And by then, hopefully, we will be to Bethlehem, and the third day's sun will rise, and with it, the Christ.

"Once he is risen, they will be unable to conjure any demons onto this plane," Gaspar said. "It will be difficult for any supernatural entities, especially those of a demonic nature, to remain here for any length of time, so long as the risen Christ walks the earth. So we will be safe."

"At least against overt demonic attacks," Magdalene said.

Gaspar nodded.

"If not against those demons that lie within the human heart," Magdalene said. "Those invited inside or created within the heart and mind."

Gaspar looked to the heavens.

"Those are considerably more difficult," he said, looking at her, "for anyone to exorcise."

TWENTY-TWO

Melchior's camp was arranged in a circle around a small fire. Philip and Andrew slept near the horse and cart, while Tanara, Melchior and Simon Peter remained awake and vigilant.

Simon Peter sat staring at a small piece of paper, and a tear brushed his cheek.

"What causes you sadness, my friend?" Melchior said.

"It is not sadness… not entirely, more a bittersweet feeling," Simon Peter said. "Love, pride, and a hope I live to see them again, a hope to make the world a better place for them."

Simon Peter showed Melchior and Tanara the worn paper, upon which were drawings and wishes of love and hope, farewells, from his children. Written and given to him the night before Christ's death, before the disciples assembled in the garden of Gethsemane.

"My son, Paul, and daughter, Bethany," Simon Peter said. "I… told them I would have plenty of stories for them when I came back."

Tanara felt her heart flood as she looked upon the words, scrawled in primitive yet passionate fashion, "Love you daddy. I love you too, so much."

"You will have many stories to tell them, for many years to come," Melchior said. "You are a man of many lives, much like your own father."

Simon Peter smiled.

"He was a good man, an amazing warrior, a man of exceptional morals and character," Melchior said. "As you remember from your own childhood, he went on many missions for the Silent Hand, and, as you will, he returned from them all.

"Your love for your family, for your wife, your children, is a strength, not a weakness," Melchior said. "It is the reason we live. We need to feel there is a reason for all of this, all of this pain, all of this suffering. And it is because in this world there is also such great beauty and love. That is our strength. That is what we fight for."

"But there is so much suffering, so much to endure, and overcome," Tanara said.

"Within us and outside us, yes," Melchior said. "But it is not who you were, or the suffering you endured that defines you, nor is it those that inflicted that suffering upon you. It is you who defines yourself. It is who you are and who you strive to become that is important."

"Is it not written in the prophecies that the Christ will rise? Does that not guarantee our victory?" Simon Peter said.

"There are no guarantees," Melchior said. "There are infinite ways in which the universe can travel. In almost all of those permutations of time, the Christ is destined to rise. But only the past is written in stone, the future, only sand. If our actions are true, we can make sure it happens in this dimension, on this mortal plane. But if we fail, if Satan is able to turn his body into the antichrist, then not only will he be able to create a hell on this earth, but the power and negative energy released by that success will ripple into other dimensions and influence the outcome, making it all the more likely that Satan succeeds on other planes as well, and rules with an ever more imposing iron fist throughout the dimensional realms."

"That is why our quest is of such importance," Melchior said. "He who refuses to see the big picture while staring at the small is he who loses his place in both."

Melchior held up the paper Simon Peter had given him, with its precious, sincere expressions of love and fidelity upon it, looked at it and smiled, then handed it back to Simon Peter.

"Such a small thing, one which could be so easily destroyed, yet one which symbolizes and which carries such power, such love," Melchior said. "We are much the same way. Fragile, impermanent, so easily destroyed. And yet filled with such power, such love, to change our hearts, and change the world."

TWENTY-THREE

It was 4 a.m.

The Hour of the Wolf.

The time when Satan's power was at its apex upon the earth.

The sky tore and screamed as a lightning bolt stabbed through the air, slamming into the earth and shattering the rock around Balthazar's camp.

Immediately, they were surrounded.

But just before the attack, the Arimathean had jolted awake, and when it arrived, he was prepared, twin swords in hand – his own steel in one, the holy blade of Soulsfire in the other.

Balthazar had already been awake, on watch, and he stood, his own holy sword, Heavensblade, in hand, raising his arms in an illumination spell to douse the night in flame and light around them, displaying the wretched creatures suddenly surrounding them, and for a moment keeping them at bay beyond a ring of holy fire.

The warriors had been shaken awake by the earth's tremors and now stood, swords in hand, awaiting their fate. The disciples, Matthew and Simon the Zealot, concentrated in the middle of the camp on either side of the cart containing the body, with Balthazar, Barabbas and the Arimathean on the front lines, in a triangular formation.

Balthazar's magicks illuminated the darkness, allowing them a glimpse at the growing throng of demons about them.

The Gundari.

Large, wolven bodies, razor sharp claws the length of daggers, tails whipping about with the stings of scorpions at their razor-sharp tips, and the faces of leeches, with three slick, slithering proboscises slathering from their gaping maws.

"They have no minds, no capacity for anything but destruction," Balthazar said. "They are ravenous, unstoppable devourers of human flesh and bone but will only prey on and eat the living and those freshly killed. They despise the taste and smell of the dead."

"So our enemy is trying to completely eliminate us but keep the body of Christ intact?" the Arimathean said.

"Exactly," Balthazar said.

"Some corpses get all the luck," Barabbas said.

They stood united, in a circle, ready for battle. Barabbas. The Arimathean. Balthazar. Matthew. Simon the Zealot. Each with two blades in hand. The Arimathean and Balthazar filling one fist with earthen steel and the other with the blue fire of soulsblades, holy swords with the power to not only slay demons but send them howling back to the bowels of hell.

Then the fire lifted, dissipating into the night and illuminating it, and the Gundari rushed in at the warriors, claws slashing at them, heads dashing in, fangs flaring at the warriors, trying to get a fresh taste of human flesh.

Simon the Zealot was a man of few words, but of obvious advantage in battle, as he feverishly and relentlessly hacked his swords away at the beasts, catching first blood as he slayed one of the first demons to lunge at them. But his anger blinded him and he yelled out in pain as a Gundari maw full of needle-sharp fangs sank into his shoulder.

Immediately, the Arimathean was at his side, dispatching his own beast and then the one which had attacked the Zealot. And behind him, Barabbas cut down another with a two bladed attack.

Balthazar's blade impaled yet another, and with a wave of his hand he sent another ring of fire about them, shoving the demons back shrieking and wounded.

"How are you?" Balthazar said to the Zealot.

"I will survive," the Zealot replied.

"Let us hope that is not merely wishful thinking," Barabbas said.

Then the fire dissipated again, and the beasts slathered in fury upon them, claws and fangs flashing in furious frenzy.

But to each attack, the holy warriors had a response, an attack in turn, and soon their might overcame the Gundari in a decimating display of power, the last demon disintegrated by the soulsblade of the Arimathean slicing it in two.

The warriors stood tall, scanning the earth and skies, as Balthazar's illumination spell continued to light the fading strains of the night, and as the sun of the new day began to approach over the horizon.

"There will be another to follow, another demon, likely a wraith or shade," Balthazar said. "The Gundari are mindless beasts of destruction, and a spell summoning them would have also included a trailing demon, to collect the body of Christ as ours were being eaten by the Gundari.

"We have passed this first test, but there will be more," Balthazar said. "We must remain on guard."

Balthazar scanned the skies.

"As I figured," Balthazar said. "We are being watched."

The Magi pointed up and in the light of the fading moon and coming day a large raven could be seen circling far overhead.

"A familiar," the Arimathean said. "No doubt giving sight to Herod Antipas safe in his palace."

Barabbas scoffed.

"How happy we are, then, to disappoint him," Barabbas said.

They remained on guard, looking about the horizon.

But saw nothing.

Nothing but the dark raven on one end of the sky, near the end of the night.

And their own familiar, the ivory owl Seraphim on the other, at the dawning day.

"Well, that was not so bad," Barabbas said.

"No," Balthazar said. "Herod Antipas and his vizier are not the mages his father and vizier were."

"They have grown weaker while you have gotten stronger in the last three decades, one would presume," Barabbas said.

He looked at Balthazar and the Arimathean. "I have often marveled at how neither of you seems to have aged a day since I first met you as a child," Barabbas said. "If only the rest of us could be so fortunate."

Balthazar gazed at Barabbas and the Arimathean.

"Less revelry upon your part, Barabbas, could work wonders," Balthazar said, with a smile.

"Ah yes," Barabbas said. "But what is a long life without living?"

Balthazar's brow remained furrowed, his eyes distant in thought.

"What is it?" the Arimathean said to him.

"This is most curious," Balthazar said.

"Perhaps the energy exerted by us as a group severed the link between the two demons?" the Arimathean said. "Or perhaps, as you said, Herod Antipas truly is much the lesser than his father and was unable to cast such an advanced spell."

"Perhaps," Balthazar said, still scanning the skies, "perhaps."

Balthazar remained troubled.

"This is unusual," Balthazar said. "I do not like it. We must be… very careful."

They gathered their things and started off again, following the Magi at their lead.

But behind them, the blackened remains of the Gundari began to emit a strange glow, a crimson mist, as they stirred, separating from one another, as tiny, clawed legs slowly sprouted, dark and sharp, from their sides.

TWENTY-FOUR

At the Hour of the Wolf, Magdalene was jarred awake, shoved into consciousness as if by some supernatural force.

She looked down, and saw as the amulet around her neck glowed with a slight ice blue, felt it warm against her skin, and then, fade to cold again.

Gaspar had already been awake and alert, on guard.

"What is it?" Gaspar said.

"I am not sure," Magdalene said. "But something, something… not good."

"Wake up!" Gaspar called out to the camp. "We must be on guard!"

But it was too late.

Seconds later, as they rose groggily, the sky rumbled and the crimson pellets, dark blood, fell from above, drenching Gaspar, Magdalene, Bartholomew, Philip, Thomas and Jude.

"Magdalene!" Gaspar cried out.

But she was already prepared for his request, throwing up an illumination spell so they could see what was attacking them.

As the droplets hit them, it produced a strange sensation as their flesh chilled and crawled and the pools of red coagulated upon them, sprouting spiked claws, long jagged legs and hungry jaws.

The illumination spell lit up the night sky, but as the first fangs newly formed cut into his skin, Gaspar knew, knew which demon had been summoned to devour them.

Oostynynthyne the Dark Sea of Daggers.

A demon collective, a swarm of beasts spawned from the loins of Satan himself, which manifested on the earth plane first as a hail of blood, but which would collect at the touch of human flesh, boiling into an ocean of ebon, red-eyed creatures, part cockroach, part spider, with needle-sharp claws and jaws.

First, the needles would jab and numb the victims, killing their flesh of all feeling as the bites began and the creatures would slowly devour and overcome them. As they bit, they were not only sucking their flesh into their gullets, but also bits of their spirit, their essence, and then spitting them back out, under the control of the demonic entity, until the victim was nothing more than a zombie, a slave, to the whims of the demon.

As the demons swarmed, they emitted a foul odor, a dark mist, which would hover about them, dripping ever more blood rain, becoming ever more of the tiny, voracious beasts, eating, eating, until nothing remained of the victims but demonic puppets controlled by the collective evil.

The warriors could not fight this demon through brute means. Their strength meant nothing. Even the mightiest of all Magi, the most powerful being upon the earth, Gaspar, was left helpless.

But not Magdalene.

As soon as she recognized the demon collective, she began calling out prayers, incantations, and even as her skin burned fire from the bites, she continued to call out the words in a desperate plea for help and a cathartic release of the pain which gripped her flesh.

She watched as her fellow travelers writhed in agony, flailing about, as they were slowly overcome, taken over. She could see them losing control of their bodies and souls. Even Gaspar, whose massive frame was driven to his knees on the rough sand as his body teemed with dark crimson death, his fists ripping massive chunks of the tiny darkseeds from his body, only to have them scramble back towards him and onto his flesh.

As she reached the last syllables of her incantation, Magdalene could feel the fangs frenzy into her mouth, down her throat, in a thousand stings. But with a powerful cough she spat them out and as her head grew light, her flesh saturated with venom, she belted out the last words of the spell, the spell she had been taught as a child, by the Revelator, so many years ago.

She breathed the last of the incantation, and she fell to the ground in agony.

But as she did, a potent burst of energy exploded holy fire within her, flame devouring and disintegrating the fangs within her and upon her skin, and then, exploding around her, burning the millions of crimson creatures blanketing her companions, and bathing them all in a warm, healing light.

They rose slowly, as the remnants of the demon whirled into a tight tornado, then down into a dark, whirling orb, which sank slowly, down into the ground.

"Are you all?" Magdalene said.

The disciples, exhausted and drenched in sweat, nodded.

"We survive," Gaspar said, "because of you."

But as they looked around them, they noticed something accompanying them which did not survive the attack.

The cart.

The body.

The wood carrier, toppled and crushed. The cloaks torn and tattered, the corpse in a ruddy state of disintegration. But enough of it remained. Enough to know.

"This was not the Christ," Gaspar said, looking over the body.

And above them, they heard a shrill sound, saw a dark shape, soar away into the distance.

Gaspar and Magdalene's eyes darted to each other's.

"We have to leave here," Gaspar said. "We have to rejoin the others. Immediately."

TWENTY-FIVE

As with Magdalene, upon the fourth hour past midnight, Melchior had been jolted awake. Not by any jewel about his neck, but through his own precognition and the uncanny link he shared with his Magi brethren.

Sensing his fellow Magi had been attacked, he called the others in his camp out of sleep and threw up an illumination spell to show, on the horizon, a portal of acrid black and putrid green ooze, opening in the firmament.

He quickly jumped his consciousness into his familiar, Cherubim, tried to glean the fate of Gaspar and Balthazar, but for some reason, he could not. All was clouded upon the astral plane across which they meant to communicate.

And just as his consciousness leapt fully back into his body, immediately he and his camp came under piercing psychic attack, their minds full of horrible scenes of abomination and perversion, making it difficult to concentrate on anything but the sickness they felt at the parade of horrors oozing through their minds.

Only Melchior remained able to turn the attack away, but he felt himself battered by its power and depravity. It was as if the demon sensed his leap into Cherubim and knew well how defenseless it left him. And so, while he remained determined, strong, he felt a growing pain inside, and was stunned at the ferocity of the attack and its ability to wound him.

But he struggled forward, as the tentacles began to drop down, the slithering intestines slathered in acid blood, from the maw of the vulgar beast hovering above them.

"The R'aall'akai!" Melchior called out.

Tanara had gained some measure of cognizance and rose to her feet to face the demon with Melchior. Having endured endless cruelties heaped upon her, she had adapted the ability to compartmentalize the evils in her mind, shove them down and away in order to function. And so she stood at the ready next to the Magi.

"What is that?" she said.

"One of the most wretched demons of the ancient depths," Melchior said. "It drives its victims to madness with its spell of perversions, then attaches itself to a human host with its lamprey-fanged arms and takes it over, to suck its flesh down to

hell to reenact those same depravities and thus scar it for all
eternity.

"It is not only here to kill and damn us, but to do the
same for the body of Christ, to pull it down to hell so that Satan
may use it as his plaything," Melchior said.

The two looked to the disciples, Andrew, Philip and
Simon Peter, but they were struggling to stay on their feet,
screaming in pain and grimacing from the attack.

Simon Peter gritted his teeth, his brow a tempest. "We…
will resist it…we… will have faith…" he said, his sword tightly
in hand.

Melchior looked to Tanara. "Our weapons are fairly
useless against it," the Magi said. "We must use magick to send
it back to hell or it will not only drag us with it, it will continue
to spread its pestilence throughout this dimensional plane and
possess all it encounters along the way."

Tanara and Melchior joined hands and between them a
halo of bright white light emerged about them, the disciples and
the body in the cart, shielding them from the tentacles which
stabbed with steely fangs into the energy sphere about them. But
then, the demon merely grew larger, larger, its arms more
plentiful, until it continued to expand across the shield, across
the desert, darkening all about them.

Tanara fell to her knees and cried out. It was too much. The demon too strong. She was a fierce wizard but she was still only human.

Only the Magi born remained steadfast. Melchior battled valiantly, but he could feel himself grow weaker, still hobbled by the demon's ferocious initial attack upon his defenseless body, and he knew he had little choice. If he allowed the R'aall'akai to remain in this realm, the demon would wreak havoc. Not only would it would abduct the body they protected, but it would be little time before it followed the energy strands of Cherubim back to the other Magi and the rest of the disciples, dooming them all to hell, and leaving Satan to rule earth with the antichrist as his slave.

He also knew if he waited any longer, he would grow weak, too weak to cast the spell, with too little life force to expend, too little of a life that was already growing dim in the face of overwhelmingly powerful opposition, one which, he knew, was too much for him alone.

And so, in a moment, he made his peace, in his mind, in his soul, knowing, knowing, this was not the end.

And then he bid farewell to the world of flesh.

Her eyes pursed in pain, clouded with tears, Tanara's glance caught the Magi's, saw the peace in his eyes, upon his face.

"No... Melchior... no!" she cried out.

Melchior smiled. "We are all fragile things, but the love we hold is strong," he said. "And there is no greater gift than to sacrifice ourselves for that love."

And within him, he began to utter the spell, the one almost certain to spell his doom, but, also, to undoubtedly destroy the demons which were already swarming about him and the others, burning away at the shield tenuously protecting them, and hungering to add their corpses to the hell fields from whence the ancient demon came.

Melchior looked to Tanara and she felt his voice in her head, calming her. Then he closed his eyes and raised his arms mightily, repeated the words, softly, then louder, over and over, and felt the flames rise within him, felt a fiery force permeate his every essence and rise from his body, enveloping him in a brilliant energy. And as he did, he began to fight with renewed strength and fury, and the shield burned brighter and the demons began to fall, fall, disintegrating and hurtling back to the limbo with every powerful swing of his arms.

Above him, the clouds opened and a beam of light lowered, until it encompassed him, and made him rage with power all the more. And the demons about them begin to falter.

Around him, the ground shook as concentric waves of energy emitted from his core, tightening about him, pulling the demons fast around his aura in a whirlpool of white and aqua light.

As the maelstrom of fangs and fire whirred around him, the demons desperately clawing to life, Melchior held fast, his body trembling, bulging with the power coursing through him, before it exploded, along with his heart in his chest.

But as his body disintegrated, his soul leaving its vessel in a halo of blue light, the last sight to fill his fading eyes was that of the evil destroyed, immolated by the explosion of his spirit, and sent spiraling back into the void, with the hellmouth sealed shut.

And then, the sky cleared and was illuminated in a bright aqua light as Melchior's body dissolved to white ash and his own spirit rose heavenward in a halo of blue flame, and streaked eastward, back to the eternal halls of the Golden City of S'iam B'ala.

As a light gray smoke rose, licked with the blood-red flames of demon remnants returning to the nether hells, the bodies of those left behind lay motionless beneath, twisted in the sand. Until one by one, they rose, coughing and caked in sweat, looking about them at the carnage left behind.

The disciples rose, along with Tanara, only to notice that the body, the one they believed was the Christ, was bathed in a strange mist.

Tanara ran to it, and moved to pull the cloak from its face.

"Wait! You cannot!" Andrew cried. "We are not supposed to…"

"Let her!" Simon Peter said. "We need to see what has happened!"

The last wrapping fell away, and they looked into the face of the man, one of the men who had been crucified next to the Christ. His eyes were hollow, his face a grimace, and a strange mist emitted from about his head.

"What…" Andrew said.

"Do you think?" Philip said.

"The demon was able to get into all of our heads," Simon Peter said. "All of them. Even this one."

He looked around at them, as they gazed upon the dead man's face.

"They know now that we did not have the body of the Christ," Simon Peter said.

He heard a sound from above.

Saw a dark figure.

As the raven looked down, its eyes glazed with a silver glow.

He looked at Tanara.

"We need to find the others," Simon Peter said.

She looked up at the sky. The night was fading, and the afterglow of Melchior's passing illuminated the firmament at the start of the new day.

And she saw, high above…

"Cherubim."

The white owl circled about them, his eyes glowing silver, one last time, before soaring, forlornly, into the horizon.

TWENTY-SIX

"What was that?" James Alphaeus said, watching as the dark figure disappeared across the horizon.

"A raven, a familiar," Magdalene said. "Its eyes a mirror to those who sent this demon to slay us."

"And if they know it failed?" Thomas said.

"And they know now that this is not the Christ?" James Alphaeus said.

"Then this is not good," Bartholomew said.

The ground shook violently and a rift opened where the dark orb had pierced the earth.

"Magdalene," Gaspar said, "we need to return to…"

"I know," Magdalene said, as she pulled the small, sigiled elements from her satchel and threw them to the ground. Once they hit the earth they glowed a strange orange light, emitting a dark purple mist. A light rose upward that Magdalene and Gaspar used to create an arc, then connected into a large oval shield of protection.

"All of you, into the orb with us, now!" she called, as the disciples leapt into the sacred space she and Gaspar had conjured.

With a tremendous upheaval, the earth split and a gigantic whirling ball of dark crimson hurtled into the sky where the black demonic orb had burrowed into the ground. Once it had reached above the travelers, the ball shattered into a liquid claw of blood, hurling down upon them.

However, it was met by a blue halo of light surrounding them, acting as an additional shield against the onslaught. The oval burned bright around the travelers and within, Magdalene held tight to the beautiful, occult amulet around her neck, which began to glow and emit a hologram which expanded into a succession of geometric shapes, opening the gate which would take them to safety.

"What?" Thomas said, then grimaced and called out in agony as the crimson stain bit his skin and quickly expanded into fangs and claws, before being crushed and burned in holy fire by the hand of Gaspar.

Gaspar looked up and saw from whence it had come.

A slow crack.

Forming in the shield above them.

One drip.

Then another.

Onto Bartholomew, causing him to writhe in pain, attempting to brush it off, but failing, until Gaspar could once more dispatch it.

Magdalene closed her eyes, concentrated, and willed the gate to open, to transport them away, faster.

But she could feel the shield about them becoming weak, weighted down, and eaten away slowly by the fist of crimson doom about them.

"The power... the power of this demon is... I have never..." she said.

Gaspar acted quickly, putting himself beneath the minute hole in the shield, flickering in and out, as the demon collective scratched and struggled to get inside, to feed. As the darklings began to make their way through, slowly, they latched upon his skin, his energy, and his teeth clenched in pain, his face reddened and twisted in determination, as the demon spawn continued to gnaw away at the shield, and stab and bite away at his flesh at every chance when the shield opened, ripping into him, slowly draining the Magi of his strength and power.

And as they gained his power, they became stronger, more furious, more numerous, more voracious, and the shield became weaker, Magdalene's spell became more unfocused and scattered, the gateway hologram wobbling with a strange sound and glow.

"What is happening?" Bartholomew said.

"We should be leaving through the nether portal, but we are not," Thomas said.

Gaspar looked at Magdalene. She returned his steely gaze.

"You cannot leave as long as they are within the shield," Gaspar said, "as long as I am with you."

He strained to push himself upward, blocking the hole in the shield all the more tightly. His eyes stabbed towards hers.

"Give me the blade," he said.

"No, you cannot," she said.

"It is your only chance," he said.

She concentrated all the more, poured herself into the incantation, but it was for naught. The portal would not fully open as long as the shield was breached, and already she could feel the weight of the demon spawn upon it, causing it to weaken. It would not hold much longer.

At her belt she concealed a blade, the remains of the spear which had pierced the side of Christ at the moment his spirit had left his body, as he died on the cross.

The spear of destiny.

Under the orders of Herod Antipas, the centurion had stabbed the body, the steel collecting its last essence, its blood of water and wine. Herod Antipas had planned to use the blade in ritual, to help transform the Christ to evil, and to use it as a potent weapon against any potential supernatural opposition. With the blood of the Christ still upon it, it had the power to dispel any evil and send any demon screaming back to the mouth of hell.

The Arimathean knew this, and after taking the body had likewise stolen away with the blade, giving it to Magdalene, in case it was needed on her journey. Only Gaspar knew she held it. Only Gaspar knew of its power.

"Give me the blade," he said. "It is the only way."

She concentrated harder, felt her essence, her energy, pouring into the incantation, but Oostynynthyne was born of the darkest depths of hell, offspring of Satan himself, and it took all of her considerable strength to even hold it at bay.

Gaspar looked into her eyes.

"He sacrificed himself for us," Gaspar said. "I must do the same for him."

Magdalene realized she had little chance and no choice.

And so, she reached into her belt, pulled from it the blade of the spear and handed it to Gaspar.

He grasped it tightly, and his face gripped like a fist in concentration, power and pain. His mighty muscles tensed and in an instant exploded, as he hurtled upwards, through the shield. His energy, augmented by the spear, acting as a magnet for the demon, pulling its millions of black, skittering claws upward and away from the shield, and swarming them to his own body.

Magdalene wasted no time. Without the weight of the demon spawn upon the shield, upon her, she welled with power. Within an instant she forced the gate open in a brilliant explosion of color and light and she and the disciples were sucked into the vortex, which glowed a bright, incandescent white. She stood at its center, then stopped, the maelstrom around her orbiting an eye of calm. She grasped the amulet around her neck, one of amethyst and onyx, silver and sapphire, an ancient icon of love and fidelity and strength, crafted and blessed by a long bloodline of warriors.

Warriors from the harsh, barren lands of Arimathea.

She clasped it, and within her, the image appeared, of the one who wore the amulet's twin, an image that became clear in her mind.

The air exploded and the vortex, in a blinding burst of light, disappeared.

But not before one last image flooded her memory.

That of Gaspar, high above them, the demons violently frenzied about him, cloaking him and merging with his essence, as he drove the spear into himself and they exploded in a ball of flame. The demonic collective hurtled back to hell. Gaspar's human form dissolved. His spirit, an outline in clear blue flame, burned high into the heavens, and back, back to the Golden City, of S'iam B'ala.

And all that remained was the blade, the remains of the spear, fallen to the ground, which quaked and rent asunder to swallow and hide it, for centuries to come.

And then the earth stilled, the sand blew over it, leaving the desert still and cold. The final epitaph of a warrior's courage, soon whisked over by brutal wind, sand and dust, left to nothing but memory.

TWENTY-SEVEN

"If we are attacked again, it will likely be from the skies," Balthazar said, as the warriors trudged through the oppressive warmth of the new day, "although it is strange to have such a time between the demons one would expect linked together."

"How so?" Matthew said.

"Demonic entities cannot survive for too long in our dimension," Balthazar said. "They are brought forth with not just blood but fear, hatred, anger, and if the blood is released with all permeating it, it is all the more potent. But that is also why they must continue to kill, to feed on the fear and suffering they generate, not only feeding on the flesh and blood of humans but the negative energy generated in that flesh and blood by the fear and anger poisoning it."

"So if one dies fighting them with courage and strength and without fear..." Barabbas said.

"The demon does not feed, or it is of limited nourishment," Balthazar said.

"Perhaps then, with the Gundari dispatched so quickly, their link to their symbiote was severed," the Arimathean said.

"Perhaps," Balthazar said.

They continued on through the day, Balthazar and the Arimathean at the fore, with the horse and cart containing the body between them, and Barabbas, Simon the Zealot and Matthew behind.

As Matthew walked, he periodically scrawled notes upon a paper and returned it to his satchel.

"What are you writing?" Barabbas said.

"Thoughts, ideas, tales of our journey," Matthew said.

Barabbas smiled.

"Knowledge is currency," Barabbas said. "And the man who writes the tale controls history."

"No," Matthew said. "Unfortunately, the man who edits the final tale controls it."

Barabbas laughed.

"Ever the cynic, Matthew," Simon the Zealot said.

"That is why I have always liked..." Barabbas began, before halting and wincing in pain.

"What is it?" Matthew said, before feeling a sting on his own flesh, on the back of his neck, and calling out in agony.

"Balthazar!" Simon the Zealot cried out, as he too, felt the stings upon his back.

Balthazar and the Arimathean turned quickly and leapt to the side of the men, writhing upon the ground. And then they saw the creatures, upon their companions, and others hurtling towards the Arimathean, stabbing into his skin, and Balthazar, whose superhuman Magi reflexes just barely dodged attack.

Far behind them, in the harsh grip of the rocky earth, the remains of the Gundari had indeed been gestating into a second demon wave, as Balthazar had anticipated. One even more strange and deadly than he figured.

Regenerating into the Nostrenemi.

Thick, flea-like creatures, the size of a man's fist, with bat wings sprung from their slick, scaly backs.

Balthazar immediately recognized the brood of metamorphic demons.

The Nostrenemi were blood-sucking parasites in need of a host. They would not drain to death. Instead, they would attack in numbers, slowly sucking the blood and life force of their victims, as the venom of their saliva invaded the blood and auric system, causing intense hallucinations of the worst memories of that victim's existence while likewise crippling their nervous system, causing horrible seizures.

Balthazar knew then, the reason for them being sent. If all went according to their foes' plan, the Nostrenemi would swarm them and render them helpless as the creatures latched upon the body they protected. In theory, their bites would chemically render the body of the Christ saturated with negative energy while also draining its remaining blood, both giving their foes a fleet of receptacles for the blood of Christ to be used in diabolical spells, and making the body all the more ready for becoming a zombie possessed by Satan.

Balthazar's mind flew to this in an instant, as soon as he saw the demons, and he threw up an impenetrable shield about the body, horse and cart, seconds before the creatures were able to latch onto them.

Then Balthazar's shield expanded, bloomed, about them, and the shriek of the Nostrenemi were heard as they leapt from the bodies of his companions, leaving them alone in a halo of white fire.

They rose, bloodied by the bites, their minds foggy and reeling, but still strong.

"Well, there is your second demon attack," the Arimathean said to Balthazar.

"Wicked little things," Barabbas said, tending to a bleeding wound.

"This is their last chance for over a millennia," Balthazar said. "They will do everything in their power to stop this from happening."

Above them an eerie black and putrid green cloud formed.

"The Nostrenemi do not kill, they paralyze," Balthazar said. "They did not want to kill us, they wanted to capture us, and the body, and abduct us through that portal."

"Why not kill us?" Matthew said.

"They wanted to turn us, the same way they wanted to turn the Christ," Balthazar said.

"But why us?" Barabbas said. "Why not attack our entire group at the beginning of our quest in such a way?"

"Because we are the only ones they think they could turn," the Arimathean said.

"Why?" Simon the Zealot said.

"Because we are the ones who have sinned the most, who have the most darkness in our souls," the Arimathean said.

Balthazar considered a moment, then looked to his companions.

"Join hands with me! All of you, join hands in a circle," Balthazar said. "Do not be alarmed at what you feel, do not unlock your hands once you have joined them!"

The travelers quickly complied.

Within their midst, they could feel a heat, like a fire, growing in intensity until it enveloped and surrounded them, and began to emanate, radiate out in a circle about them, devouring the Nostrenemi, gnashing about in spasms of hunger and hate, thrashing forward futilely against the circle of fire around the warriors, until finally the flames engulfed the demons and they succumbed, and they were sucked upward into the gaping maw of the hellmouth, which closed shut and disappeared with a brilliant flash.

The enemy defeated, Balthazar raised his arms again and called back the sacred fire, and it subsided back into their circle, before dissolving and disappearing among them.

"So we are safe?" Matthew said.

"We are safe… for now," Balthazar said. "And for some time, to allow us travel."

"How much time?" Matthew said.

"Probably at most twelve hours," Balthazar said. "It will take some time for them to conjure up another demon."

They heard a sound from above.

"What is…?" Matthew said.

The travelers looked to the skies.

"It is of no worry," Barabbas said, "it is merely the owl. Seraphim."

"No," the Arimathean said, "it is not Seraphim."

Balthazar looked closely.

"No, it is not," the Magi said, pointing to another spot. "Seraphim flies there."

The Magi pointed back. "That… is Electrum."

Suddenly, as if a veil were lifted, Balthazar could feel himself at one with the familiar, looking through its eyes, and seeing… what had occurred.

And with the visions seen through the eyes of the pale familiar still haunting his mind, Balthazar's head slumped, his heart dropped and he turned to his companions.

"Gaspar… is… no more."

"What?" the Arimathean said.

"Gaspar… he sacrificed himself to save the others…" Balthazar said. "I do not know… somehow we were disconnected… our links through the familiars were severed… that is… not impossible, but…"

The two owls circled overhead as the travelers felt themselves suddenly much, much less confident than they had mere moments before.

"Are the others dead as well?" the Arimathean said.

Balthazar paused, used the strength of his will to access the memories of the familiars, but felt it far more difficult than it should have been.

"I cannot tell," Balthazar said. "The information is locked to me."

The Arimathean's face froze in a mixture of shock and sadness.

"These are not the magicks of a decrepit shadow mage like Antipas, nor his faded vizier," Balthazar said. "These are Roman signatures, of the highest order. Empowered… by Satan."

And then, in the sky, they saw a light, a growing orb of illumination, moving towards them.

"What is that?" Matthew said.

"I do not know," Barabbas said. "But it is not a bird."

TWENTY-EIGHT

The light in the sky grew stronger, closer, began to emit
a strange, high-pitched sound, as it glistened with a panorama of
color.

"I am guessing this is not good," Barabbas said,
unsheathing his sword.

"When has it been?" Matthew said.

But Balthazar, snapping from his grief, dispassionately
watched as the glowing sphere grew larger, and closer to them.

And as it did, the amulet about the neck of the
Arimathean began to warm and glow.

"It is not a hellgate," Balthazar said, "I can feel it does
not bear evil."

"It is Magdalene!" the Arimathean said.

The sphere touched down in the sand nearby them and
expanded into a brilliant, multi-colored array of elaborate
geometric shapes, and as it did, the bright white oval at the

middle opened up, and the shapes began to dissipate. And as they did, the figures appeared, until only they remained.

Magdalene, Bartholomew, James Alphaeus, Thomas and Jude.

The gateway flashed and disappeared in a pink mist, and the travelers, gaining their bearings, sighed and enthusiastically greeted Balthazar and the rest, with warm embraces.

"We thought you had been lost!" Balthazar said, his arm around Jude.

"No," Jude said. "We escaped, we live, because of her. Her, and the sacrifice of…"

"Of Gaspar," Balthazar said, with heavy heart and breaking words. "We know."

"What of the others?" Bartholomew said. "Have you heard?"

"We can only guess," Barabbas said. "We know nothing. We did not know if you were alive or dead until you walked from that portal."

"But how? The familiars…" Jude said to Balthazar.

"I am not sure," Balthazar said. "Roman magicks, of a power I have rarely seen, and one which has seemed to be able to cut us off from one another, and from even the familiars."

The Arimathean held Magdalene tight to him, kissing her tenderly, and they separated themselves from the others.

"You could have died," the Arimathean said.

"But I did not," Magdalene said, glancing down at the amulet about her. "I survived. Thanks in part to you."

He looked at her, at all of her, and it sunk into the depths of him how close he came to losing her, forever.

She looked into his eyes, burnt earth and gold, and realized how close she had come to seeing them nevermore.

They kissed, tender and long, flowing into one another, and when their lips parted they gazed deep into each other's eyes, breathing deeply, softly, in the heavy air of the coming dawn.

His hand moved tenderly curving across her cheek, through her hair, his eyes never leaving her.

"I know," she said, her eyes returning his. "I know."

She looked at him, into his eyes, intensely. "But you cannot always fear losing me, you cannot live in fear of my death," she said. "This is the life we have chosen, the risks we take as warriors. Every time we step onto the battlefield we can be defeated. Every time we lead others into battle, we can die, as can they."

"I know," the Arimathean said. "That is why I lead none but myself. I am not Balthazar, I am not Melchior, or Gaspar. I am a leader on none but my own path."

"You are right, but you do not lack the power or the courage or the wisdom to lead," Magdalene said. "You only lack the faith. You fear the mantle of leadership, for you fear being responsible for losing any who might follow you.

"But you are a leader, whether you realize it or not," Magdalene said. "You lead in your actions, your integrity, your courage and strength. Even in your solitude, others look to you for guidance because you are the one who does not surrender. You are the rock, the one who stands strong against all and refuses to let the world around him, let the evil around him, change his path.

"Look around you," she said. "Look at us. Me. Tanara. Barabbas. You have led us all whether you have wanted to or not. You have led us in your kindness to us, your protection you gave us, the path you helped set us upon. We looked to you for example on how to follow that path with strength and integrity. We are all misfits in our own way. All of us fighting against our own demons, our own battles, on our own paths. Sometimes being a leader is not about leading others along one path. It is showing them the courage and strength it takes to inspire them to travel faithfully on their own.

"You did not lead us as one above us, treat us as subservient to you, you led us as equals, you took your path and told us, through your actions, that we could take the same,"

Magdalene said. "You had faith in us. We had faith in you. Have faith in yourself. Have faith in us all. Have faith in me."

The Arimathean thought for a moment, letting her words sink into him, and then he looked to her.

"I do," he said.

She put her hand around his shoulder, let it roam around the back of his neck.

"And so you should have faith in yourself, not only for yourself, but as a leader of others," she said. "Of that I am certain. As certain as I am of my feelings for you."

He looked into her eyes and they embraced.

Barabbas watched the two of them from a distance, smiling and nodding to them, then to Balthazar.

"That surprises me not at all," Barabbas said, of the pair. "Like attracts like."

Balthazar smiled. "That is one of the secrets of the universe, my friend," the Magi said.

"Which is why I find myself alone with drink," Barabbas said, raising an eyebrow, and a flask to his mouth. "Strong, dark and equal harbinger of joy and sorrow."

"You are not so different from him, you know," the Magi said, nodding towards the Arimathean.

"But we are," Barabbas said. "For he is the man I wish I could be, and he wishes he could be almost anyone but himself."

Barabbas drank deeply, and Balthazar was silent, his eyes slanting in thought, as he looked to the Arimathean and Magdalene, and then, up, at the blossoming daylight.

TWENTY-NINE

They continued on through the day, following the path to Bethlehem, while anxiously awaiting any word on the others. At the fore of the group were Balthazar, the Arimathean, Barabbas, Matthew and Jude. The others fell behind, surrounding the horse-drawn cart, and the body, still wrapped in the violet shroud.

"I did not anticipate attacks of such power and complexity," Balthazar said. "I figured this to be the best plan of safeguarding the body."

"It has been," the Arimathean said. "And it will be."

Balthazar looked to him, with a slanted gaze, and he could tell. He could tell the Arimathean was, if not aware of his plan, then certainly piecing it together.

"Where do you think they are?" Barabbas said, interjecting. "The others…"

"It is… difficult to say…" the Arimathean said.

"Melchior is a powerful Magi," Balthazar said. "Nearly as powerful and I. And those among his camp, Simon Peter, Tanara, the others, are skilled warriors. We must have hope they still survive."

"And what… what of Gaspar?" Barabbas said.

"His body, the body of a Magi, does not remain once it has expired on this plane," Balthazar said. "It is a hollow shell, a vehicle, and once shed it disintegrates. His spirit remains, and has returned, to the higher planes, of the Glowing City."

"Will it not rise to heaven?" Jude said.

"It may," Balthazar said. "But a Magi is of a different breed. Our souls travel amidst different worlds and occult dimensions of time and space. In time, Gaspar's being may reside in heaven. Or it may remain amongst our brethren in the ethereal worlds of the Golden City. Or it may return, someday, in some other incarnation, to earth, if he is needed, or if he wishes."

Matthew stepped forward. "Is that what would happen to us?" he said.

"Humankind is very different than we Magi," Balthazar said. "For you, heaven will be your just reward. When the time comes."

"And what of the other body with them, the one thought to be the Christ's?" Barabbas said.

"It was a body with a spirit long left behind," Balthazar said. "One which had left its body, to go… I know not where."

"Who was he?" Matthew said.

"It was of one of the men killed beside the Christ," the Arimathean said. "One I saved from a much worse fate than being lost and buried amidst the desert."

"And so the two other bodies, the ones not the Christ, are of those killed beside him?" Barabbas said.

The Arimathean and Balthazar traded quick glances.

"Two of the bodies carried among our parties are, yes, the two bodies of the men killed beside Christ," the Arimathean said.

"What is that?" Barabbas cried out, again pointing to another figure in the sky approaching.

The Arimathean felt an iron mallet to the chest as he recognized it.

"Cherubim," the Arimathean said. "The third familiar."

And again, the visions flooded into Balthazar's head, the last scenes of battle, and the death of the other Magi, Melchior. The death of his other dearest, closest friend.

"That is Melchior's familiar!" Barabbas said. "Does that mean Melchior as well?"

Balthazar nodded, silently, shaken.

"They," he said, with a heavy sigh, "they are both gone."

THIRTY

Uncertain of what to do or where to go, but knowing the other travelers would be headed to Bethlehem, Simon Peter led Tanara, Andrew and Philip towards that city of Christ's birth, hoping to reunite with their companions.

Their leader, Melchior, was dead, having sacrificed his own life to save them.

Cherubim, their familiar, and ostensibly their connection to the groups led by the other two Magi, had mysteriously abandoned them.

And the body they were protecting, which they had believed to possibly be the Christ, was revealed to be one of the criminals crucified beside Jesus, a ruse utilized to confuse their enemies.

Enemies which now knew they did not have the Christ.

Enemies which now knew they were undefended by a Magi.

And enemies which could and would likely attempt to eliminate them before they could rendezvous with the others to help them on their quest.

None of the group knew what had happened to the others. None of the group knew the master plan, or which of the three teams protected the actual body of the Christ. They were only instructed to go to Bethlehem, to rendezvous there by dawn on Sunday.

None of them had the power to conjure a stargate, or to transport to the side of their companions, and only Tanara had any experience in the trek between worlds. Simon Peter had only read maps and theories on the dimensional portals. Andrew and Philip were barely aware of their existence.

And so, lacking any other options, they continued on, following their path to Bethlehem.

It was near sunset when they saw it appear in the sky.

A bizarre, oscillating light of bright green and a putrid fleshen color, which quickly descended upon them and opened like a wound, dripping slime upon the earth, and pouring forth from it an army of severed limbs which slithered together upon splattering the ground, forming an array of grotesque figures.

"What is that?" Philip said, terrified.

"What do we do?" Andrew said, echoing his fear.

"Draw your weapons and get behind us," Tanara said.

"And if you have charms, if you have any enchantments to throw to protect yourselves or us, now is the time to do it," Simon Peter said.

"Do not fear it!" Tanara said, turning to the pair. "Or you will have already lost!"

"It is the demon collective Syylavius, a mass of beasts from the depths," Simon Peter said, as the grotesqueries shambled towards them. "Each of them has the body of a man crossed with a serpent, claws of a lion, tail of a scorpion and eyes and a gaping maw like a lizard's, but emitting razor-sharp claws and tongues slicked with stings like a wasp. It exists to bring us pain, to saturate our blood with the venom of terror, before it peels our flesh from our bones."

Andrew and Philip froze in horror. They had seen battle against warriors, centurions, even half-demon humans, but they had never seen anything like this. And the fear in them was seized upon and augmented by the demon, which sensed it and used its power to spread that terror throughout their being, ripening them for its hunger.

But Tanara and Simon Peter stepped to the fore, knowing full well that the beasts could sense that fear and were feasting upon it, gaining strength from it, drooling over the prospect of human flesh filling their gullets.

"This is not a demon meant to possess or capture us," Simon Peter said. "This is a killing machine meant to destroy us."

"There is no more need for pretense or subtlety on their part," Tanara said. "They know this body is not the Christ's, and they only mean to eliminate us all."

"And they will, unless we act quickly," Simon Peter said. "For we are little match for demons of this level, especially as they feed upon the fear of the others."

"But how will we..." Tanara said.

Simon Peter looked to the gate, just past the demons, then to Tanara.

"We have no idea..."

"Exactly," Simon Peter said. "So it is uncertain death or certain death. Which would you prefer?"

The beasts were nearly upon them, and Philip and Andrew began to whimper as the demons hissed in pleasure at the delicious feel of their fear, and began to attack them psychically, fouling their minds with the visions of their disembowelment, demise and devouring at the hungry claws and maws of the hell spawn.

"It is our only chance," Simon Peter said.

Tanara nodded, and with one hand upon her sword, her other went to a secret compartment within her belt.

She released a small vial of indigo powder into the air and it whirled as it created a vortex of sparks and prisms about her and her companions, a shield of light which, for the moment, dispelled the storm of demons, causing them to shriek in agony. It would not last, but it did not have to, if they moved quickly.

Simon Peter, as he had been instructed, so many years ago, as a boy in the mystery schools, threw a handful of sigil-carved charms to the ground and uttered ancient prayers and the dimensional portal from which the demons emerged was pulled towards them, past the array of gnashing claws and teeth, until the gate was before them, a glowing portal.

To where, they did not know.

"You still have the soulsblade the Arimathean crafted for you?" Simon Peter said to Tanara.

"Arantioch, yes," Tanara said.

"Hold tight to it," Simon Peter said, "Do not let it go under any circumstances, and within your mind, hold even tighter to the thought of the Arimathean, as will I. In crafting a soulsblade, one leaves an imprint of themselves upon it. The Arimathean's imprint is upon Arantioch. If we concentrate, God willing, we will be pulled to wherever he is."

Tanara nodded. She sheathed her own steel and unsheathed the golden blade.

The gate glowed before them, and as it did, the shield about them fizzled and weakened, disrupted by the energy of the gate, and the demons swarmed towards them, slashing at it, looking to jab their talons and jaws through as it faltered.

"Quickly! Hold my hand!" Tanara said, grasping Simon Peter's outstretched arm as they locked themselves together and she tensed to leap into the gate. Simon Peter turned to Andrew and Philip.

"Quickly! Grab ahold of my hand! Both of you! Hold tightly to each other's hands and to mine and do not let go!"

The two were frozen in fear.

"Quickly! You have to have faith, or surely you will die here!" Simon Peter said.

Simon Peter winced as a demon tail whipped through the shield and buried its stinger into him. For a second he loosened his grasp upon Tanara's hand, but then grabbed it again and held tight.

"Andrew! Philip! Quickly! The shield is falling!" Simon Peter called, but the disciples remained petrified.

A demon tail slashed through the barrier and past Tanara's head but she was able to fend it off with the soulsblade. Another whipped at Simon Peter and sliced a chunk of flesh from his thigh but he was able to fight it off with his own steel.

"We have no choice," Tanara said. "The shield is about to fall! We have to go, now!"

"Andrew! Philip! Now!" Simon Peter yelled, and finally, the disciples stirred to action, leaping towards Simon Peter, and as they did, the shield was destroyed. Tanara lunged at the dimensional portal and it sucked her in, and with it, those connected to her.

But Andrew and Philip had taken too long.

Tanara and Simon Peter entered the chaos of the pathway between worlds cleanly, her right hand clutched tight about the soulsblade, held close to her heart, her left hand locked in Simon Peter's right. Simon Peter's left hand held Andrew's, and Andrew's held Philip's, but the latter two had lingered far too long before leaping into the portal, and along with them, clinging to their legs and clawing their way up their bodies, were two of the demons.

A glow emitted from the soulsblade as Tanara could see, in her mind, clearer and clearer, the Arimathean, walking through the desert with the others, and she felt herself and her companions drawn towards him, faster and faster. And as they were pulled, she saw the abominations around them, the demon beasts between worlds, which remained invisible to those on the earth, but which constantly bit away at the holes of the human mind, burrowing, trying to find a way to parasite into the psyche.

She felt a thousand tiny stings as their tongues lashed at her, and she knew her companions felt the same, but she could see nothing, she knew nothing, of what transpired behind her. She could only feel the weight of them, could only feel the strength of Simon Peter's grip about her hand, and could feel his own energy, his own faith, making her stronger, as she felt the Arimathean grow clearer, clearer, in her mind.

And then, it stopped.

There was nothing.

Total silence.

Complete nothingness, only brilliant white, as if staring at the sun.

And time missing.

Later on, she would have no memory of what had happened to her then. No idea of what had happened to her, or her companions, between worlds. When she emerged, she bled with fresh wounds, disgusting gashes upon her skin, but she would have no memory of how they got there. She only knew that she had gotten them during the journey between the dimensions.

The last she had remembered was the feeling of energy about her, the vision of the Arimathean in her mind.

And then, missing time.

Then the feel of an earthquake, of the world shattering around her, closing in upon her quickly, and then, she saw an unearthly green glow, and then the earth, again, as she tumbled from the gate to see the Arimathean there before her, as she had seen in her vision.

As Tanara and Simon Peter fell to the ground, Balthazar galvanized his energies on closing the hellgate behind them. Already the slimy gray tentacles of demonic entities began to slither through the neon green ooze of the portal, but they were quickly sent shrieking back as Balthazar's body rippled with lightning and he sealed the mouth.

Tanara and Simon Peter collapsed on the ground, covered in mysterious wounds. Balthazar raised his hands above them as Magdalene and Jude joined in for prayers of recovery, washing a healing white light over them until they stirred and sat up.

They looked around, at those before them, at each other, and then around again.

"We…" Tanara said, gasping for breath, dripping in sweat, "are the only two that remain?"

"You are the only two that emerged from the dimensional portal," Jude said. "Were there others that entered with you?"

"Andrew… and Philip…" Simon Peter said, still trying to catch his breath. "They entered with us… did they not make it through?"

Magdalene looked to the ground, then up, again to them.

"You were the only ones," she said.

THIRTY-ONE

They stopped to rest as evening fell, and the camp was divided in three, each group keeping to themselves, about the fire.

Balthazar and Barabbas. The former awake on watch, the latter having fallen asleep.

The disciples and Tanara. Some asleep, others with eyes shut, trying in vain to sleep.

And the Arimathean and Magdalene.

They sat alone, apart from the others, and he held her in his arms as she slept, before shaking awake.

"The nightmares again?" the Arimathean said.

"Yes," she said.

"The same?"

"Yes," she said.

He caressed her hair, held her to his chest. His fingers wandered her shoulder gently, down her arms, to the scars on her forearms.

The scars she had held since childhood.

She was young, barely a girl, when her parents were slain, and she was taken.

Taken by a particularly virulent Roman commander who looked over her area, whose soldiers purged her people in a much less random fashion than the fattened, greedy prefects of old. A Roman commander bursting with an enormous appetite for the young, the unclaimed, male and female, to slake his unholy thirsts. He would accuse their parents of false charges, imprison or slay them, and steal the children away, to keep in a perverse harem, toys to his whims.

And so she was marked unclean.

But still, she remained undefiled.

From birth, she was possessed of magicks, a power, beyond her, that even she did not comprehend.

One which followed her will.

Which imparted a force upon others.

Which protected her.

Each time the commander approached her, he could not take her, and she remained undefiled.

Frustrated, he branded her a witch, a whore, and in fury carved letters in her arm.

WW.

Letters which she would later transpose.

And take as her name.

To replace the name she could not remember.

To replace being called "it."

WW. Facing outwards on her arm. The letters as presented to the world, for its interpretation. But facing inwards, towards her, waiting for her interpretation, her creation, MM.

Mary Magdalene.

She remembered, her childhood, the nights, the nightmares, the sounds of others, not so fortunate. And when she did sleep, she was haunted and transfixed, praying for a gateway to her freedom, a night she could find her place, her hope, in this world.

It arrived in the guise of a tall, gaunt, man in black garments, wearing a strange mask of onyx with a darkly tinted visor over his eyes, and three crimson slashes across his mask.

He was a powerful mage, and carried with him twin weapons -- gigantic, silver, four-pronged stars of mighty, glimmering blades, which he used as swords and which he could throw with enough force to slice a soldier in two in an instant, only to have the blade return to his hand, caught with reflexes faster than any living being she had seen before.

The man descended upon their camp one night.

A man who called himself John.

And others called the Revelator.

He descended upon their camp, she thought, in answer to her prayers.

And on that night, the screams she heard were not of children.

But of their tormentors.

She woke, and watched, as he destroyed them, cursed them.

"These are human beings, not the playthings of animals," the Revelator scowled, as his steel hovered over the sweating, panting disease of a human clenched in his fists. "Remember that, you subhuman scum, as you are defiled by the beasts of hell."

With one swift, clean swath, she watched as the man who had killed her parents, who had tortured her for what seemed like her entire life to that point, was gone.

When the Romans were slain, the Revelator took the children with him, nursed them back to health, kept them safe, and eventually they were taken in by others, good men and women who provided them with new homes, new hope, new love.

All but her.

She remained by his side.

Remained his own child.

His pupil. His protégé.

He sensed in her the power she had barely sensed in herself. He helped her develop it, control it, hone it, and trained her to use it, to use it for good, much as he used his own.

She was raised by him, raised and educated through the mystery schools of the Silent Hand. Mentored by the Magi. And, eventually, by the Arimathean as well.

She had first met the Arimathean more than three decades prior, on the journey to safeguard the parents of the Christ, to protect them on the way to Bethlehem, so the Christ would be born.

Since that time, she had grown, grown to adulthood, become a woman.

But during that same time, the Arimathean had not aged.

Not a day.

He remained the same. The same man she had met three decades prior.

She did not know why, or how, but somehow, she had aged beyond him.

When they met again, decades on, their relationship took on a decidedly different dynamic.

Of equals.

Partners.

Friends.

And, more.

"I never knew my father, nor my mother," Magdalene said, softly. "I have only truly loved three men in this world. John, like a father. The Christ, like a brother. And you."

She looked into his eyes.

"And you, like no other," she said.

And like comets colliding, they exploded into one another, holding tight, bodies and lips inseparable and insatiable, burning and brilliant, incandescent, slaking their need until it had calmed and they could once more feel safe as one, knowing and calm.

They held each other softly, laying still, entwined and warm, as the fire burned low and danced shadows across them.

She kissed him softly, slowly, then their lips gently drifted from each other, their eyes still entwined, open.

She looked deep into his, their bodies still and enveloped in each other's, their hands clasped tightly together.

"I wish I could have been there, I could have saved your parents, I could have saved you," the Arimathean said.

"I know you do," Magdalene said.

"I do not need you to save me," she said. "I need you to walk beside me. Together we can face anything."

She laid her face upon his chest, his hands gingerly running through her hair, as she gazed out into the night.

"Anything."

THIRTY-TWO

The crystal before the three flashed silver, relaying the images in the eyes of the ravens above each battlefield.

"And so they unite with Balthazar, who carries with him the body of the true Christ," the Judas-Satan symbiote said, with a smirk. "And there we shall crush them."

Pilate and Tiberius likewise smiled, and watched, as dark figures began to emerge from the pit of blood within the palace throne room. Figures that were all familiar, but twisted and perverse. And as each rose, they were armed with Roman steel and weaponry of the demonic arts.

Once they had all emerged, Judas, his eyes crimson fire, his body filled with the power of Satan, stood at the fore of them, and raised his arms, and as he did, the glowing putrid green hellmouth above them began to lower, slowly, to envelope them and send them hurtling to war with the holy cadre.

Just before entering the portal, Judas turned to Tiberius and Pilate with a growl.

"Find the mother of the Christ, find her while I kill them and bring his body back as my slave," Judas said. "She will make a fine queen for me, to breed a new lineage of power."

And then Judas turned, cackling with a cold-blooded hack, and leapt into the portal, which rose, again, to hover above the room, above the gaping maw of sacrificial blood.

"Should I dispatch a fleet of centurions?" Pilate said, nervously.

Tiberius scoffed.

"There is no need," the emperor said. "It is already done. As are they."

Tiberius strode to a large, ornate box on the opposite end of the room, a box which had been unloaded after his arrival, and one which he had visited periodically during his stay. As with his other visits to it, he took a key from his belt and opened it. But unlike his other visits, this time, he lifted the contents out, brought them to the throne, and placed them on a small table alongside it.

It was a large rectangular object, a golden tray, with sides riding upwards as if an arena.

And within it was a wooden board, upon which ornately carved pieces were exquisitely placed.

On one side, the pieces were carved in onyx.

On the other, ivory.

A few pieces, more ivory than onyx, were scattered alongside the board, obviously removed from their regular places upon it.

Tiberius smiled as he plucked a few of each color, a couple of the larger pieces of each.

"Remember, Pilate, what I said about the importance of creating opposition among your enemies?" Tiberius said, with an oily smirk. "The easiest way to control your opponent is to subtly coerce him into making the move that will benefit you the most, and lead him into doing so of his own free will."

Tiberius picked up two of the large ivory pieces, looked them over and set them beside the board.

"Do you know how to get what you want, Pilate?" Tiberius said.

"Force your will upon someone?" Pilate said.

"No," Tiberius said. "That only works in the small picture, the short term, and is best between two people when you have a measurable advantage in power."

"So how then?" Pilate said.

Tiberius began removing more ivory pieces, then stopped, and began removing those from the onyx side.

"You create a problem for which what you want is the only solution," Tiberius said. "Then you introduce the problem, preferably in secret, or subtly, and you watch as someone else embraces your solution and takes action to give you exactly what you wanted all along."

Pilate watched as Tiberius considered the board.

"Pilate, who is your deadliest foe, the only one from which you cannot escape?"

"I… am not sure…" Pilate said. "The will of the people? Those closest to you?"

"No," Tiberius said. "Yourself. Only you truly know your greatest fears and weaknesses. And only you can deceive yourself so thoroughly as to your power and pride."

Tiberius picked up a large onyx piece.

"And as we know, pride goes," Tiberius said, "before the fall."

Tiberius took the large, ornate onyx piece and set it aside the board.

He smiled, and looked over the strange tapestry of pieces.

And then he turned back to the crystal which once more began to mist and glow in a silvery haze.

THIRTY-THREE

After a brief respite for the weary travelers, Balthazar led their way through the night, the Arimathean and Magdalene just behind him, scanning the horizon, as the others lagged behind, pulling the cart and flanking it for protection. They carried torches to light the way, but in truth the night was brilliant with stars and a heavy moon which loomed ominously over them.

"I cannot believe they are all gone," Jude said. "The Magi, Philip, Andrew… I cannot."

The disciples bowed their heads.

"They will be remembered, and spoken of in tale, and written of in valor, to honor the sacrifice they made," Simon Peter said. "They will never be forgotten."

"Indeed," Matthew said. "In truth, we will write of their legacies with such fire and tribute it will be as if they never died."

"In our hearts, they never will," Thomas said. "They will be remembered, wherever we go."

"Wherever is an apt term," Barabbas said. "For this quest seems to have taken an eternity in less than three days' time."

"This seems an odd quest to me," Bartholomew said. "I understand that Bethlehem offers refuge and holy protection, but not until Christ's rising, which would offer us protection anyway. In the meantime, we have been little but targets, so our location would seem to be irrelevant. Why did we not just stay at the tomb or at some other location?"

"And allow them to send their full forces at us knowing full well where we are, and letting us face both human steel and sorcery?" Matthew said. "I would prefer to be moving ducks rather than sitting ones."

"But at least then we might be prepared, we might be able to set traps or gain advantageous positions, knowing when and how we face attack," Bartholomew said.

"And then we might also have more certainty as to the location of our future graves as well," Barabbas said.

"Always with the clever words, Barabbas," Thomas said. "You will have no shortage from which to choose for your epitaph."

"Have faith," Simon Peter reassured them. "This is a wise plan. It would take too long for them to send troops out to battle us, so our only enemies are those of a sorcerous means. And as those adept in the ways of magick are aware, it is best to fight those battles within a neutral environment such as this, especially one which offers so many distinct vantage points."

"What do we do next, Balthazar?" Barabbas said. "What fresh hell can we expect to face, now so close to Bethlehem, and when will its spires begin to protect us? What is our next move?"

"Our next move?" Bartholomew said. "You act as if this is some sort of game."

At once, Balthazar's eyes lit up.

"It is," the Magi said.

"What?" Barabbas said.

"This is the work of Emperor Tiberius, an emperor of great power and strength, but also one whose reign has been dictated by an uncanny logic and cunning," Balthazar said. "He is known as a lover of games, and the wisdom of these attacks, of choosing these specific demons in this specific order, only reinforces that. He is playing this as a game, with each of us, and his minions, as pieces on his board."

"And so what move do we make next?" the Arimathean said.

"The one he will not expect," Balthazar said.

THIRTY-FOUR

The early hours of Sunday coiled about the travelers until the jaws of the Hour of the Wolf opened to greet them.

In just a few hours, on this third day, according to the prophecies, the Christ would rise from the dead, along with the sun.

Balthazar, awake and watching over their camp, with the Arimathean alert and by his side, knew this final passage would be their most difficult.

He had no idea what hellish array of demons Tiberius would summon forth, but he knew it would be devastating, and he knew it would be relentless.

The Roman Emperor had already shown himself capable of incredible dark magicks, sustained enchantments and ancient demons from the lowest reaches of the abyss.

Balthazar and the Arimathean had spoken, in low voices so as to not wake or alert the others sleeping, throughout the night. But as the 4 a.m. hour loomed, the Magi girded themselves for battle.

"Wake the others," Balthazar told the Arimathean. "Time is short."

The others were roused and they began the trek, the last moments of their journey, to Bethlehem not far in the distance.

And as expected, they were not alone.

Just past 4 a.m., it began.

The skies clouded over the night, a gray hand grasping the horizon, and a vortex of blackened wind and green slime stabbed down from the sky and exploded upon the earth.

Balthazar threw up an illumination spell and the earth and skies were alight, allowing them to see what emerged from the maw of the vortex.

A cadre of warriors, faces pale and sallow, cut and wounded, but all too familiar.

Them.

Or rather, zombified versions of each of them.

Created from the blood and energy leeched by the Nostrenemi that attacked Balthazar's camp. And as such, the zombified doppelgangers of those in Balthazar's camp who had been directly bled – Balthazar, the Arimathean, Barabbas, Matthew and Simon the Zealot – bore an uncanny resemblance to them, with little more than the ashen skin and chapped wounds marking the difference. As for the others -- the disciples, Magdalene and Tanara -- their darkling mirrors were created from the energy signatures and memories of those directly bled, and then the blanks were filled in with demon flesh. So their mirror images were anything but, and were instead a grotesque mélange of themselves crossed with the mutated and awful figures of hades.

And at the lead of the zombie army, a familiar figure.

Judas Iscariot.

Indwelt by Satan.

"And so we meet again, for the last time, for you," Judas growled, as he led the hell spawn forward in battle. And as he did, the holy warriors could feel their mirror images' psychic attacks, stabbing into their heads. They had been created, formed in the sacrificial pit, mined from all of their sins committed, all of the guilt and self-hatred felt, by the holy warriors. And as the zombies attacked, once more the holy warriors could feel those transgressions and their own sorrow and self-loathing for their actions, and it dipped their souls in acid, distracting them, as they struggled to fend off the jagged weapons of their evil doppelgangers.

The disciples, wracked by the burden of their pain and doubt, felt their strength sap from them, and the zombie versions of themselves began to gain the advantage. The sound of steel on steel clashing in equal measure began to be replaced by the cries of pain and struggle as the disciples fell back, losing strength against the relentless shades of pale.

But not all of the holy warriors felt such a disease of the mind.

Balthazar, pure of thought and deed throughout his life, was immune. The Arimathean and Magdalene, having suffered so much already, having made peace with their own sins as toll for their suffering, were bereft of that crippling guilt. Likewise, Barabbas, who justified all of his actions within his own defiant logic, was not affected. As such, their doppelgangers were far weaker than they, mere hollow shells of attack, and were quickly destroyed.

But the other disciples, already doubting themselves, found themselves battling both within and without.

Balthazar sensed this and within the disciples' minds they heard the Magi's voice, calming them. And within the minds of the Arimathean and Magdalene, Balthazar's voice was also clear, instructing them on what to do.

Balthazar, the Arimathean and Magdalene uttered the same prayers, again and again, forming a trinity, and energy flowed between them, forming a halo about them that spread out and over the disciples, clearing their minds and purifying their thoughts.

The disciples felt themselves reinvigorated, strong, and once more the sounds of steel clashing rang through the air, this time interspersed by the sickening thunk of those same weapons finding demon zombie flesh and crippling their enemies.

But one enemy was not so easily defeated.

Judas.

THIRTY-FIVE

The warriors battled fiercely against the decrepit, pale versions of themselves, twisted and turned by Satan into hollow shells of hatred.

The zombies were tireless and strong, relentless in their attack, but they were slow and methodical, powered by loathing and terror, and after the trinity spell anchored by Balthazar, the disciples felt themselves renewed, cleansed, and that rebirth sapped the power of their demon doppelgangers, allowing the disciples to destroy them.

The last of the zombies had been defeated.

And only Judas, possessed by Satan, remained.

The Satan-Judas symbiote continued to clash in battle with Balthazar, the mightiest of the Magi. The demon-human's ebon hellblade, Lucisfang, slashed forward in a frenzy, seeking to destroy the Magi. Balthazar's blue flamed sword, Heavensblade, blocked its every attack, as their battle edged closer and closer to the cart and shrouded body, until they were right next to it.

And as Balthazar noticed the others had emerged victorious, the Magi feigned weakness to his foe. With a herculean swing, the demon's sword smashed against Balthazar's soulsblade, and Balthazar allowed himself to be driven back through the air several feet, faking injury, knowing the temptation of absconding with the shrouded body would be too much.

Just as he thought, as soon as he flew back, out of range of Judas' weapon, instead of Iscariot moving in for the kill, the betrayer bounded towards the cart Balthazar had been guarding.

Grasping the body, Iscariot immediately summoned the hellgate downward, and it began to spiral quickly to him. And for a moment, the flesh of Judas quaked and blistered as Satan began to leave the body of Iscariot to leap into the latent form wrapped in cloth, the body he believe to be the Christ's.

But then… he realized the truth.

He felt the auric signature of the body.

And he knew it was not the Christ.

Judas was stunned for just a moment, unsure of what to do, and his hesitance cost him.

Balthazar surprised him, and as the spiral of the hellgate hovered just overhead, Balthazar leapt at him and drove the golden blade Arantioch, which he had retrieved from Tanara, into the body of Judas.

The golden dagger's power was such that it would dispatch the soul of a mortal man, or a lower demon, to limbo, banishing it until it was released by a higher power. Balthazar was uncertain exactly how it would affect Judas, especially since Iscariot was indwelt by Satan, the most powerful of all demons. He had anticipated it sending the soul of Iscariot to limbo and Satan back to hades. So as he stabbed the dagger into the man-demon's chest, he called out a prayer of exorcism, an ancient prayer meant to banish demons back to hell.

Judas' body shook and Satan within it lashed out in pain and anger as the body began to blister with heat. The hellgate whirled around them and then engulfed Judas, causing his body to seize with greater violence as Balthazar held the dagger within him, calling out the prayers again and again, louder and louder over the din of the raging hellmouth.

"If I go to hell, I am taking you with me!" Satan growled, as a series of black, scaly tentacles ripped from the flesh of Judas' body and whipped endlessly around Balthazar, wrapping him up as the vortex took them both.

"Yes, you are, and I will make sure you do not return to this realm," Balthazar said, allowing himself to be pulled into the hellgate.

And as he did, he smiled to the Arimathean, and in his head, the Arimathean heard the voice of the Magi.

"The greatest thing any person can do," the voice of Balthazar said, serenely, "is sacrifice themselves for others."

Judas and Balthazar struggled against each other, battling to the last, until with a massive explosion of light and sound the gate closed, taking Balthazar and the Satan-Judas symbiote with it.

Through the dimensional gate.

And down, down to the bowels of hell.

THIRTY-SIX

With the vortex evaporated and the hellgate shut, the desert was quiet.

The body, the one they thought was the Christ, the one the Judas-Satan symbiote had just held in his arms, attempting to possess it, lay on the ground, still.

The Arimathean walked to it, unwrapped the cloth from its face and shoulders, and was unsurprised at what he saw.

James.

Unaware, unawake, in a Kuti, an Eastern state of deepest meditation, in which the body is kept alive in suspended animation for almost three days, between life and death, allowing it to travel the astral plane.

Only the Magi and those within the innermost circles of the Silent Hand were aware of the practice.

But James, being the brother of the Revelator, being one of those who walked between worlds, would be able to achieve such a state.

From a distance, no demon or mage would be able to identify the body, due to the amethyst charm about it. Even at close range, they would, at most, and with great expense of power and ability, be able to tell that it was within that state of suspended animation, and if they had detected that, they would think it was the Christ. Only by direct contact with it, and thus its auric field, would they know it was not the Christ.

And so they had fooled their enemies.

Until Satan himself, perhaps the only demon with the power to detect the auric signature of the Christ, was able to have physical contact with the body.

Balthazar had anticipated the shock of discovering the truth would allow him an opening to surprise the Judas-Satan symbiote, and banish it to hell.

He was prepared to drag it there, if necessary, to save the others.

Magdalene stood alongside the Arimathean, and gasped as she saw the face of James.

"You have known all along?" Magdalene said to the Arimathean.

"I suspected," the Arimathean said. "Only Balthazar knew. Until last night. Until just before the last attack. Just before you woke. He told me what he was going to do, and what we needed to do once he did, if he had to end up sacrificing himself."

The Arimathean leaned down, placed his hand upon the forehead of James, and uttered an ancient incantation, three times. A halo of energy passed between and around them, and then James' eyes flickered, and he woke.

"Are we… did we succeed? Has the Christ risen?" James said.

The Arimathean shook his head.

James sat up, his shoulders slouched.

"We are still a few hours away from his return," the Arimathean said. "There is no time to explain. We need to return to him. And we needed you, awake, to do so, to lead us in the space between worlds, and take us with haste back to the one with whom you are linked."

"The body," Magdalene said, the realization now clear, "is still in the tomb."

"It is," the Arimathean said. "It has been all along. This quest, our trek, has been nothing but a diversion. Balthazar did not even tell me his plan, until he had to. He never would have if he did not have to potentially sacrifice himself to eliminate Judas. He did not want to risk the body being abducted at all. He wanted the enemy to be overconfident and focus solely on us. And it would have worked, had it not been for the power and cunning of Tiberius' attacks and the immersion of Satan into the fray.

"Ready the enchantment," he said to Magdalene and James. "Open the gate. I will rally the others to return to the tomb."

They nodded.

"We will get through this," he said to Magdalene, his voice steely and sure, his hand on her shoulder, "together."

"We will," she said, with a slight smile. "And we will lead them, together, back to where we must go. To see this through to the end."

THIRTY-SEVEN

Tiberius smirked as he hovered over the crystal, watching the battle unfold and end. High above the battlefield his raven familiar had flown, and through its oil eyes, through dark enchantments, the Roman emperor had seen it all, and it had unfolded precisely as he had planned.

He walked from the throne to the gaming board, and removed two large pieces, one ivory and one onyx, and paused to contemplate as he held them in his hand, before putting them face down on the side of the board and turning to Pilate.

"Through spies, sorcery or intuition, they knew that your plan was to allow them to tomb the Christ's body," Tiberius said. "They knew it would make you feel safe, that you were placating the masses while being able to keep tabs on it in a secure location. They also knew, or figured, that in order to insure that, you would install a fleet of troops around the tomb.

"Then they led us on a journey miles away, hoping to distract us, hoping to make us think that they had stolen the body, hoping to keep our eyes on them, luring us to them, away from the city," Tiberius said. "And they thought that even if we had discovered the truth about them not having the body, that we would think the body was ensconced in some secret hideaway of the Silent Hand, which would lead us to scramble to find it, thus distracting us even further, until beyond the third day, when the Christ would rise."

"And so that was their plan?" Pilate said. "The body is hidden in some clandestine location underground, some hideaway for the Silent Hand?"

"No, you fool, that is what they wanted you to think," Tiberius said. "The body is actually in the last place you would look, the last place they would think you would look, the place you would believe, and perhaps the only place on earth, you would believe to be totally and completely secured by you. The tomb. The body never left the tomb."

"But our soldiers looked inside it and the body was gone!" Pilate said.

"It is not inside it," Tiberius smiled. "It is underneath it."

Tiberius bounded to the throne and sat before the crystal, concentrated and muttered occult spells, and watched as it glowed silver, and that glow was matched in his eyes.

"What are you doing?" Pilate said.

"I am sending a piece of my sentience across the astral plane, into a familiar nearby the tomb," Tiberius said. "And through that familiar, I will command those centurions guarding it to begin looking for a secret pathway to another tomb beneath it. There they will find the Christ's body, and his mother, and they will bring both of them to me."

Tiberius smirked, but then, suddenly, his face became a mask of shock and pain.

His body began to quiver and spasm upon the throne.

His eyes rolled up white in his head.

He writhed to the ground, and as he did, the crystal glowed brighter, and brighter, until it began to pool crimson within it, and turn dark, dark as the color which now occupied the eyes of Tiberius as he raised up his body, and with a fanged smile turned to Pilate.

"Tiberius, you are a fool," Satan's guttural voice growled from the lips of the emperor. "You thought you could deceive the prince of lies? You thought you could trap me and see me banished to hell so you could rule this earthly plane? And then you thought you could engage in black magic without opening your soul up to me? Both you, and Balthazar, were foolish to underestimate my power, and now, you shall make a fine host for me…"

Pilate's face froze in fear.

"Pilate, begin the sacrifices and ritual once more, at greater pace, until you drain every drop of blood in our coffers!" the Satan-Tiberius symbiote said. "Our centurions will strive to find the body, but I have summoned forth an even more powerful army, fueled by our blood sacrifices, to make certain they do, and to make certain that the Christ will not rise, unless it is as my servant."

The Satan-Tiberius symbiote laughed.

"The Christ will die once more and be mine!" the demon-human cackled. "And he will be his own engine of destruction!"

THIRTY-EIGHT

The blackling dropped from the night, and with a scratch of claws on steel, the raven perched upon the Roman commander's shoulder. In the soldier's head, he heard the voice, the voice of Tiberius and Satan conjoined.

"At arms!" the commander called out to the centurions assembled around the tomb. "By order of the emperor Tiberius, we are to take the tomb!"

The soldiers stood for a moment, surprised.

"But..." one of them asked. "We did not..."

"Yours is not to question, officer!" the commander shouted. "Yours is to follow my order! And I order you all, remove the stone, and look for secret passageways in the ground or walls! We will ransack the tomb until we find the bodies we seek! Those of the Christ, enshrouded, and his mother, the traitor to the throne. Take them both, alive, and bring them to Tiberius at the palace, upon my order, and order of the emperor himself!"

The soldiers did not question further. They bolted to action, pushing the huge stone aside from the entrance, and entering the tomb, swords in one hand, torches in the other.

"There is a hidden passage, leading to a space beneath!" the commander said. "Find it, and find them, and bring them to me!"

The soldiers entered the tomb, but as they did, their bodies fired back out the entrance, bloody and dead, pushing the wave of centurions back.

As emerging from the tomb were two men.

Both tall and lithe, wired in muscle and clad in black garb that stretched tight about them. Their faces were shielded with onyx ceremonial masks. Each bore three red slashes across their mask, and the headgear cloaked their eyes with strange, darkly shaded visors that made them look like demons from the darkest pits of hell, or archangels bringing vengeance down from the gates of heaven.

In each of their hands, they held massive four-pronged, silver swords that shimmered in the firelight.

The centurions stepped back a moment in fear. They had never seen such warriors.

They had never seen the likes of John the Revelator, and his apprentice, Matthias the Bold.

With the troops surprised, the two figures sheathed in black wreaked havoc upon them, slicing through their number before many of them could even lift their swords in defense. The centurions recovered and battled potently, Roman steel slashing away in an attempt to slay these two wraiths which moved like lightning among them, dealing death in their path.

But ultimately, even four dozen Roman troops were little match for the elite power and speed of the warriors of the Silent Hand, the sentinels of the body of Christ, and they stood victorious over the centurions, each scanning the heavens, waiting, waiting, for another attack.

The Revelator pointed upward, at a glowing star in the sky, one which grew larger, larger, and moved nearer, nearer.

Matthias clenched his fist and girded himself for battle, but the Revelator assured him there was no need.

As the bright light appeared, it glowed with a cascading array of colors and geometric shapes as it lowered gently to the ground. The Revelator raised his arms and from them shot lightning and white light as he opened the gate, allowing the travelers to pass through.

The disciples. Magdalene. The Arimathean. Tanara. Barabbas. And the Revelator's brother, James.

The Revelator closed the gate and it shot up into the sky like a comet, leaving the weary occupants behind, as they embraced in reunion with John and his apprentice.

The Revelator and Matthias removed their helmets, and John embraced his former apprentice, the one he loved like a daughter.

"It is good to see you again, to see you alive," the Revelator said to Magdalene.

"And it is good to say the same of you," she said to him.

"The body, the Christ, and Mary, they remain?" the Arimathean said.

"Safe, yes," the Revelator said. "Still safe, hidden in the catacombs below."

The Arimathean nodded.

The Revelator looked around them.

"Where are the Magi?" he asked. "Or the others?"

Magdalene looked down. The Arimathean shook his head.

The Revelator was stunned.

"Even the Magi?" the Revelator said. "How?"

"They sacrificed their all," the Arimathean said. "As they would have, three decades past."

The Revelator nodded, saddened.

But they had little time to mourn.

They knew the hour of the dawn was near. The time when the Christ would rise. And so they knew that this would be their last stand, in these waning few hours. They replaced the front stone of the tomb, sealing it, and stood, as one, on guard until sunrise.

They knew that Satan would stop at nothing, nothing at this point, because he had everything to lose.

THIRTY-NINE

In the occluded crystal, on the dais of the throne, Pilate and Tiberius watched the battle unfold.

They watched as the Revelator and Matthias emerged victorious. They watched as the others joined them, and were now by their side.

Pilate simmered in frustration. But Tiberius, still with Satan burning inside his body, possessing him, remained calm, amused. And once more he maneuvered the pieces about his gaming board.

"Excellent," Tiberius said. "We have only moments before the sun rises and the Christ will resurrect, but we now know all. They have revealed themselves. They have revealed the full extent of their plan and their power, and now, we will reveal ours, and it will crush them until their bones are powdered, and the Christ himself is throne to my whims!"

"But how?" Pilate said.

The Tiberius-Satan symbiote laughed.

"Through those enchantments brought forth from the energy we have drained of this pit of sacrifice, and all of my own power on this planet," the symbiote said. "I am Satan, and for these last few moments, as the Christ remains between worlds, my reign on this earth is at its peak. The Christ is in limbo. He cannot re-enter the earth's sphere until daybreak, but he has already freed the souls of purgatory and hell that he promised to redeem. But in doing so, in this window as his earthly followers wait for his return, the portals between worlds are open and in flux, because of the Christ. And so I shall shove wide the gates of hell and unleash an army of the damned, at my command.

"And what is more, I will be able to retain control and possess not only this fool's body, but a triune of hosts," Satan growled through Tiberius.

"A triune?" Pilate said.

"Three bodies," Satan hissed. "The three most depraved and dark-hearted of men, each enthroning me in their hearts, each a conduit to my power! Tiberius, Judas Iscariot, and, one other… one other which I shall shed when the Christ's body becomes available to me.

"They will all be unleashed, released from hell, brought to the tomb by hellgate at my command. Even now the gate masses above the tomb, above these pathetic fools, as we speak. And my army of the damned will destroy the resistance once and for all, shatter the entranceways of the tombs and present the body of the Christ to me, to possess and reanimate as the antichrist, thus condemning the soul of the Christ to limbo forevermore!"

Pilate sneered, satisfied.

"Remember, Pilate, it is always darkest," Satan growled through the lips of Tiberius, "before the dawn."

FORTY

The heavens ripped asunder and the earth was whipped raw as the lightning stabbed down, torrents of rain bleeding in its wake.

And in the distance the holy warriors saw a shooting star, a putrid green glow, come smashing down into the ground not far from them.

Standing sentinel at the entrance of the tomb, the holy warriors could see the hellgate, enormous and grotesque, slither from the crater. With a bursting bubble of slime and ooze, the gate and the storm broke upon the dirt in the distance, and a mass of figures began to emerge and frenzy towards them, towards the tomb, and towards their destiny.

Magdalene's spell had brought illumination to the sky and earth, allowing them to see their attackers, but it was both blessing and curse.

A sea of twisted, jagged, dark entities armed to the teeth approached, cackling and gnashing their teeth in anticipation of the battle, in anticipation of blood.

The lost souls of hell.

Allowed one more chance to walk the earth, in service of Satan, to carry out his will.

"The Christ has succeeded in his mission, to free the righteous souls of purgatory," the Revelator said. "However, Satan has followed in his path, and has freed the wicked souls of the lower realms, no doubt with promise of their conquest of us leading to their taking over the earth, again, with him as their leader."

"At least we can gain solace in knowing the Christ has succeeded in his mission, and those souls of purgatory have found peace in heaven," Jude said.

"Small solace that we may be joining them before long," Thomas said.

The Arimathean was silent, his teeth clenched, his brow turbulent, as he saw, at last, one lost soul leading the army of the depraved.

He was a monster of a man, at least a foot taller than any of the others.

Armor dark and sleek, like a cockroach's coat, and exploding with spikes of steel still soiled with the gore of his kills.

Skin death pale, a sharp, rat-like nose and jagged teeth, with eyes black as a shark's.

The half-man, half-demon son of Herod and a succubae.

The one who had slain his wife and children.

The one he himself had killed and sent to hell.

Herodius the Defiler.

And beside him, another, who they had just seen seemingly defeated and sent to hades.

Now returned.

Still burning with the fires of demon bile within him.

Judas Iscariot.

And emerging with them, by their side, they saw them all, an army of the most vile.

Herod. Herod Antipas. Caiaphas. The men whose faces burned in Magdalene's nightmares and those whose wounds still scarred the body of Tanara.

All ignited with the dark Roman magicks of Tiberius, the power of the blood sacrifice of six-hundred and sixty-six times six, and the will of Satan.

All brought to life with one goal, to bring the body of the Christ to Satan, to turn it into the antichrist, to create the one that would lead them as they conquered the earth.

The army of the damned surrounded the tomb.

And all that stood between them and the body were the last living disciples.

Magdalene. Tanara. Simon Peter. John the Revelator. James. Matthias. Bartholomew. Thomas. Jude. James Alphaeus. Matthew. Barabbas. Simon the Zealot.

And the last one alive who had been the Christ's guardian from his birth.

The Arimathean.

And as the waning moments of the night clung like diseased claws onto skin, and the demons readied to swarm forward, the Arimathean stood before the last disciples, his sword raised, and spoke.

"This could be the last night, the last moments, of our lives," he said. "We face them, the same way the Christ did, against relentless forces of incredible power and cruelty.

"And yet, like Him, we do so for a cause. The same cause. The belief, the fire, the desire for this world to be better for our sons and daughters, for mothers and fathers, for our families and friends, for all.

"For love.

"For the belief that this is a world of love, a world of God, and not just some plaything for the spawns of Satan used for their own amusement, dangling over the angry fires of hell waiting to fall in.

"This is not their world! This is ours!

"And we will fight and die for that cause and know that if we die, we die for the right. The right way to live. The right way to be. We know that if we die, we die for the will of God and we will be reborn, we will live again. And we will fight on, for the rights of others, of all, to live their lives in peace and love and safe from the tyranny of those who would steep them in pain and shame and suffering.

"The man in this tomb, this dead man, lived his life in peace and love. He loved all, he accepted all, because he knew we are all created in God's image, we are all equal in God's love.

"And they killed him for it. They killed him for daring to say God loves us all, God can heal us all if only we let him.

"That is a message that can never die, for truth can never die.

"He told us he would rise, he would be resurrected, and we believe in him. We would not be here now if we did not.

"We may die tonight. We may be defeated. But they will not win. Because we know he will rise. We believe in the power, the love, the will of God. And we believe in the faith that can overcome all.

"If we die tonight, we die knowing our lives were not in vain, that we will rise again, that his message will never be defeated. We will die knowing that God's love will never end. If we die tonight, we die in faith, in hope, in love, the same way this man died for us!

"For God, for faith, for love!"

The disciples, hearts filled with fire, raised their weapons and shouted to the night as the demons poured forward.

But one warrior remained silent.

One warrior remained calm.

One warrior knew, knew of the danger they faced, knew of the stakes of their defeat, and knew that it would take more than the inspired words of a leader to find victory.

And within his heart, silently, for the first time in decades, Barabbas prayed.

FORTY-ONE

The demons swarmed upon them, a sickening, thrusting morass of weaponry, claws and teeth, decaying flesh and blackened limbs, singed and leathered by the flames of hell.

The disciples stood their ground and battled passionately against the onslaught of demons and condemned souls, some of them soldiers and criminals, disgusting shadows of men whom the disciples themselves had once dispatched.

But now returned, returned to earth, through the gates of hell, newly opened by Satan.

But for all the demons slain, ever more attacked, and even with mere minutes away from the rise of the new day, the night seemed an unending eternity.

The Revelator and Matthias battled mightily against the two Herods and a fleet of Roman centurions.

Tanara and Simon Peter faced off against Caiaphas and the men who had once held her captive.

The Arimathean battled Herodius, possessed by the power of Satan, with the same viciousness with which they had once fought over the birthplace of the Christ.

And Magdalene and James faced off against the man who had betrayed them, and the Christ, the man who was now one of three thrones for Satan on earth, Judas Iscariot.

Herodius, filled with bloodlust and glee, stoked by the power of Satan, frenzied at the man who had slain him more than three decades past.

"I delight in the delicacies of your wife and children in the pits of hell," the Herodius-Satan symbiote growled with a grimy smile. "We both do!"

"They live only in the halls of heaven," the Arimathean said. "Your only company is scum like you."

Their weapons exploded against each other, steel and mystical swords, causing the world to quake as a scalding hatred fueled their battle. But Herodius, in the pit of his core, could sense that this was a different warrior than the one he had faced so many years before. He could feel his power. He could sense no fear in him. And he felt, even with the might of Satan within him, the same poison of doubt and fear that once overcame him in the shadow of this warrior.

Satan burned all the more in the heart of Herodius, to overcome his trepidation, and the battle fired on, two volcanic forces refusing to yield to one another.

As across the field of battle, Satan's other symbiote faced its own challenge.

James and Magdalene were two of the most potent mages on earth, but Judas, imbued with Satan's power, guile and strength, began to overcome them.

With a blast of hellfire and burnt blood emitted from his mouth, he sent James flying backwards, and surprised and stunned Magdalene.

Disoriented by the scalding, blackened blood rising around her, trying to use her magicks to combat it, Magdalene was helpless against a more conventional attack. Judas took advantage, sending a wave of poisoned shuriken sailing at her. Her senses were attuned enough to whirl at the last minute, blocking almost all of them with the steel of her swords.

Almost all.

But not all.

And as two lodged in her thigh, she felt herself grow weary, her legs collapsing beneath her, as the wave of blood fell upon her. Judas cackled maniacally and leapt, sword in hand, to run her through, but the Arimathean, having driven Herodius onto his back and away from him with a muscular blow from his holy sword, saw Judas' attack and with a burst of sorcerous blue flame from his holy sword, Soulsfire, sent the body of Iscariot flying backwards, away from Magdalene. Judas recovered, but James had as well, and they clashed in battle.

With an explosion of light emitted from a sacred spell, Jude had turned the demons about him to ash, and rushed to Magdalene's side, raised his hands above her and began bathing her in a bright orange and gold healing energy.

"Leave me, the demons will soon be upon you," Magdalene said. "This is hopeless."

"Nothing is hopeless," Jude said, and with a final bolt of energy, she felt the poison drain away from her, felt herself filled with a holy fire. "I was not only trained by my father as a warrior," Jude said, "but by my mother, as a healer."

"And you will join both in death!" the decayed soul of Caiaphas growled as it lifted a mace to crush Jude and Magdalene.

Jude threw up a shield of protection, but it went unused, as Caiaphas' zombified form jerked backwards, dropped its arms to its sides and coughed up blood, falling to the ground, once more slain by the blade of Tanara.

"Stay dead this time, you scum," she said, as Caiaphas' remains disintegrated.

Across the field of battle, Judas slashed James aside once more, wounding but not killing him. James recovered quickly and moved to engage Iscariot, but his path was blocked and he found himself battling a horde of demon souls.

With James preoccupied, Iscariot once more pounced to attack Magdalene.

But Tanara stood between them, fending off Iscariot's attacks until Magdalene could return to the fray and the two of them battled against the demon-possessed traitor, ferociously and courageously, until a wild swing by Iscariot sent Tanara flying to the ground.

Magdalene, reinvigorated by Jude's healing spell, was able to raise her weapon and fend off the evil Iscariot before he could administer a death blow to Tanara. Again and again, their steel clashed, weapons smashing against one another in frenzy.

Magdalene refused to yield to Judas, but the power of Satan within him was too much, too powerful, and as he slashed his swords together they emitted a burst of flame that threw her backward, hurtled her across the battlefield and left her writhing in pain. Only the strength of her mystical shield kept her from death.

But in the time Judas had used to defeat Magdalene, Tanara had regained her strength and was upon him, her twin swords ripping through the air, cutting at Judas. He cackled maniacally as he parried her blows, and looked, looked, for an opening, waited, waited, for her passion to become her undoing.

Tanara continued to attack, her teeth gritted, her eyes aflame, as she envisioned herself defeating Judas. She watched as he slowly backed away from her advances, seemingly retreating. But she found herself frustrated as even her most powerful blows were met by his steel and deflected away.

And with every thwarted kill, her bloodlust grew.

And within Judas, Satan could feel her anger, and he drank of it lustily.

It was only a second, only the briefest moment in which her fury overcame her, but it was enough, enough to throw her off balance and allow Judas an opening, which he did not hesitate to take, and in one thrust, his steel was in her. And then, when she stopped, stunned, his second sword found her as well, and her arms dropped, her weapons fallen, and she slumped to the ground.

"Oh, Tanara," Judas said. "You should have heeded your messiah."

She continued to struggle, to hold on to life, struggling to reach her swords, but Judas kicked them away.

"Now, what was it he said, again?" Judas smirked.

He touched his chin in feigned confusion.

"And it was so catchy, too," he said. "Now what was it?"

Judas feigned shock at recalling the words of the Christ. "Oh yes!"

He lifted his sword above Tanara.

She looked up, helpless, to see the darkness in the sky start to fade, and she knew, she knew, that sunrise was nearly upon them, and she smiled.

"My God…" Tanara said. "My God…"

Herod brought the sword down. "He who lives by the sword…" Judas said.

Tanara looked into the eyes of the heavens and smiled.

"My God…" she said, "into your hands, I command my spirit…"

Tanara's eyes closed, the smile still upon her face.

And she breathed her last.

Judas thrust the steel down.

"…dies by the sword!"

The metal impaled Tanara, but in truth, she was already gone.

Judas leaned over her body, smirking, and began to kneel down to it, to whisper some unmentionable evil to her freshly slain corpse.

But as he did, he was nearly driven into the ground as the fire of Satan within him flickered and raged unexpectedly.

Dazed a moment, he saved himself only at the last second, as he raised his weapon to defend himself from a thunderous attack from above.

He hurtled himself back, away from his attacker, then spun onto his feet, swords at the ready.

And he knew.

He knew why Satan's anger flared.

Flared at the death of his other symbiote, Herodius.

At the hands of the man now facing off against Judas.

At the hands of the Arimathean.

FORTY-TWO

"Look into the eyes of evil, Satan, once bright with your spirit," the Arimathean said, lifting the severed head of Herodius. "And see the death you will suffer."

The Arimathean threw the head towards Judas, watched as the hatred and anger of the devil himself scalded in the crimson eyes of Iscariot, and steeled himself as the two exploded into each other. The last strains of the night erupted with lighting quick slashes of earthen steel and otherworldly blades – Judas' hellsword, the Lucisfang, emitting a blood-curdling shriek each time it clashed against the blue flame of the Arimathean's holy blade, Soulsfire.

The demon-human symbiote tried to enter the Arimathean's head, tried to poison him with doubt, hatred, guilt, fear, but it could not. The Arimathean was impenetrable and unshakable in his determination, his strength.

His closest friends died, sacrificing themselves for this cause.

The woman he loved was almost killed by this man, this demon.

His family, his world, had been destroyed and defiled and demolished by the venom of Satan, and he knew this was his chance to not just avenge them, but to realize their deaths were not in vain, that their suffering would not be repeated by others.

He could defeat Satan. Balthazar had told him, the night before, of his power, of his destiny, and he believed. In his heart, he knew.

He only needed to keep him at bay, until the Christ's rising.

And he knew, he knew, he could emerge victorious.

Their battle raged as around them the others continued to fend off the attacks of the demon armies, steel and sorcery exploding in conflict in the last waning moments of the night.

And above it all, this battle, between man and demon, between hellsblade and soulsblade.

With a maniacal laugh and a powerful tear through the air, Judas sent a killing blow at the Arimathean, but the human was too fast, and was ready to return fire. The Arimathean's soulsblade swung past, but in dodging it, Judas had miscalculated his movement and the Arimathean, the most skilled swordsman of the earthly planes, made him pay, as his second sword, his Arimathean steel, sliced hard against the side of Judas' face, drenching it and his shoulder with blood. Only the superhuman reflexes of Judas, augmented by the power of Satan within him, prevented him from being beheaded.

But the pain and the indignity of having been wounded, was enough to drive Judas and Satan into a frenzy.

The demon-human symbiote became filled with rage, pain, overconfidence, and he attacked in a blur, as the Arimathean calculatedly fought off his attacks, again, and again, until he saw his opening.

And then the Arimathean's soulsblade landed hard and deadly into the body of Judas, and with the voice of Satan himself, he cried out in pain and jerked backwards, away from the blue light which had begun to engulf his essence and banish him back to hades.

Weakened, but still powerful, and refusing to yield, Judas laughed as the Arimathean advanced to deal the killing blow, only to be thrown back by a vortex of force that erupted about the body of Judas, sucking in the dark souls of those who had been killed on the field of battle.

The Arimathean watched as the wicked visages of his just-slain enemies – Herod, Herodius, Caiaphas, Herod Antipas -- slithered about the body of Judas and whirled into a dark cyclone about him, giving him new power. His enemy would now be host to a legion of the condemned, at the command of the

most powerful entity still burning within the body of Iscariot –
Satan himself.

The oil-charred vortex containing the souls of the just-
slain tightened, and wrapped around and thrust into Judas' body,
and his eyes glowed blood red, his teeth now fanged, his body a
slickened black like the underbelly of a viper.

But the Arimathean held no fear in his heart.

They were moments from daylight.

If he died, he would die on this field, would die for a
cause.

And he would die giving his last breath for the side of
good.

And when he did, he would die a Magi.

He spoke the words, said the secret prayer of the Magi to
himself. The mantra, three times. The same words he had sworn
he would never say again, decades ago. He thought of the three
who once walked with him between worlds – Gaspar, Melchior
and Balthazar – all passed before him. He thought of his wife
and children, his child's blanket still snug within a pouch at his
belt, his most cherished possession. And he thought of his life,
and he had faith that if he died, he would not reach his end here,
nor in hell, but instead in a better place, among those who went
before him.

And so, with strength of spirit, and strength of faith, he ignited his holy sword anew. Soulsfire erupted in blue fire in his hands, and he leapt into battle against not only the most deadly and insidious foe he had faced, but the most deadly foe humanity had faced since the earth's beginning.

Satan.

Now legion, conjoined with the diabolical souls of his enemies.

Made flesh in the body of Judas Iscariot.

FORTY-THREE

Above a heaving landscape the color of bile and blood, a wriggling morass of disgusting, ashy, bat-like creatures with veiny, translucent wings carved the air. Their thrusting pockets of flesh belched a sick, puking sound across the horizon as they shoved the beasts' horrible, distended gullets across a sky of ochre and gray, scratched by the moans of dead souls blistering in welling clouds of flame.

The sounds of whips and shrieks scarred the air along with a nauseating stench, as corpses, spent by demons of torture, fell fresh to the ground, to be kicked by excrement-caked hooves and devoured by creatures of nightmarish grotesquerie.

Cracking the clouds, came a blinding illuminant, violet and rose and gold, and the figure of a woman, clad in white and silver warrior's robes, breathtakingly brilliant, floating so slowly, descending almost imperceptibly, from the rift in the heavens.

As she wafted downward, her luminosity was an umbrella to the sky and ground and caused its bleakness to fade, as if covered by gauze, slowly, slowly, to white, and clear.

The agonized wails turned to sighs. The ground heaved open and the demons and harpies fled into the diseased womb of their demise.

As the woman bent to touch down, she opened her mouth, and, looking into the face of a man, lying chained upon the charred stones of hell, with eyes endless and clear and the color of amethyst, she sang a soft sound to him. He leaned upward to hear it, to take it in, and he smiled and looked above.

Above.

Into her soothing visage.

And beyond.

To a familiar figure, a man, a calm, gentle man, with the slightest smile, descending, arms spread, outreached, slowly, slowly, gliding down from the heavens in a blinding light.

And then, there was a whiplash of lightning and the woman and the man in the blinding white robes soared upwards and the skies closed and crackled with innumerable colors, and the man chained to the ground felt his shackles disintegrate, felt his wounds heal, felt himself drawn up with them, after them, into a whirlpool which shook him and whipped him about, until blackness enveloped him.

Silence.

Stillness.

And finally, light.

FORTY-FOUR

Empowered with the legion of darkened souls and with the might of Satan himself coursing like fire through every fibre of his being, Judas was a hurricane force. He erupted with fury upon the Arimathean with superhuman speed and strength, his blades whirling, near-missing the flesh of the Arimathean, as he drove the human back, back, with every mammoth blow.

The Arimathean remained a rock, refusing to yield, dodging or stopping every attack.

Until Judas saw his opening.

Using his sorcerous power, he pushed the Arimathean back, then lifted a stream of demon warriors from the fray and sent them hurtling at the Arimathean, distracting him and pelting him from behind.

The Arimathean fought them off quickly, slaying them, but with that moment's distraction, Judas took advantage.

With two mighty swings, he knocked the swords from the clutches of the Arimathean, and drove him hard down to the rocky ground, stunning him for a second.

"And so, the guardian dies!" the Judas-Satan symbiote scowled, as his unholy sword sliced down at the Arimathean.

With the power of Satan boiling within him, Judas' ebon hellsword fell violently at the neck of the Arimathean. But before it could send him to his death, it was halted, mid-air, with a tremendous explosion of force, by another holy sword of blue fire.

Heavensblade.

"Balthazar!" Judas shrieked.

Balthazar shoved the blade aside with all his might, sending the Judas-Satan symbiote tumbling backwards.

The Satan-Judas symbiote recovered and pounced upon Balthazar, driving the Magi backwards and exploding flame from the body of Judas, sending the Magi reeling.

But Balthazar's emergence had given the Arimathean precious time to recover. He spun away, stretched out his hand and willed the scabbard of his holy sword to fly into his grip, and then he flew upward, onto his feet, the blade of blue flame igniting.

Soulsfire in hand, the Arimathean leapt towards Judas, and as the flames of Satan rose to stop the attack, they were absorbed and swallowed by the Arimathean's holy sword and sent back into the body of Judas, scalding it and causing Satan to unleash a blood-curdling cackle as he was smashed backwards, against the rock of the tomb.

The demon-human lifted his sword to attack the Arimathean once more, only to feel the skin of Judas begin to smolder again, this time not of Satan's doing.

"What?" the symbiote growled.

He turned, and screamed in anger as he saw the first rays of sunlight stab over the horizon.

The Arimathean could feel his strength grow as the sun began to rise, and he could feel the demons' hold upon the earth begin to weaken.

He attacked Judas with all of his might, a relentless force, the holy blade of Soulsfire slashing away, battering the ebon hellsword of Satan, until with a massive, thundering blow, Soulsfire smashed the demon symbiote's sword away, leaving the heart of Judas exposed.

With one muscular thrust, the Arimathean buried the blue flame of Soulsfire into the chest of the demon symbiote and held it, impaling the body against the entrance stone of Christ's tomb, which had begun to glow brightly.

The body of Judas shuddered violently with Satan's dark energy as the blue light of Soulsfire burned within it, the

Arimathean's fist tight around its scabbard, his muscles iron as he held it tight, impaling his foe and bathing the black soul of Satan in holy fire.

The earth began to shake as the sun rose on the third day, an orange and golden glow burning over the battlefield, charring the flesh of the symbiote creature of Judas and Satan.

And then, with one last blood-curdling scream, Satan could hold on to his human throne no more.

In his last second in Judas' body, he shot a glare dripping with hatred at the Arimathean. Eyes red as blood met the dark sienna orbs of his conqueror.

"We will meet... again..." Satan growled, and a bloody smirk smeared across Judas' face.

And then, with an unholy shriek, a stench of sulphur and a knife of black smoke that stabbed down into the earth, Satan left the body of Judas Iscariot, left it dead and hollow, as it began to disintegrate to ash, blown in the winds whipping across the battlefield.

The earth shook, the sun was now full and huge over the horizon, and with a mighty heave, the glowing stone placed before the tomb fell aside, disintegrated in a blinding halo of light.

The warriors, exhausted, watched, as Jesus emerged, slowly, as he had thirty-three years prior, in nothing more than swaddling clothes, his arms around his mother, overcome with tears of joy at the sight of her son, alive again.

Jesus looked upon his disciples. He raised his face to the heavens, and smiled.

Simon Peter beamed with joy, looking at the Christ, and to his companions.

"A new day begins!" Simon Peter said. "A new era, begins!"

FORTY-FIVE

The disciples joyfully flocked around the risen Christ, and the new day was buoyant and ripe with happiness.

The battlefield and its demon occupants had disappeared, disintegrated, and in their place, a bounty of flora had bloomed upon the land.

The disciples marveled, smiled, were filled with amazement and ebullience, looking around at the Christ and each other with wide smiles.

"Where is Barabbas?" Matthew said.

They looked around, and Barabbas was nowhere to be seen.

But the Revelator looked to the Arimathean, and the Arimathean looked away, off into the distance, knowing, knowing the path upon which he had traveled, the same which Barabbas now traveled as well.

"He has left us," the Arimathean said, "to find his own destiny."

The Revelator considered, then knew, and he nodded, in resignation, and silently sent a prayer to the one who had fought beside him.

The Arimathean likewise held the same prayer, the same hope, in his heart, for the man he considered friend, the one he trained as an apprentice, the child he had once saved.

He hoped.

He prayed.

But he found his spirits dampened as he looked about them, looked about and thought about the devastation wrought, and he considered all who had not seen this sunrise, all those who had not lived to this day, both those who accompanied them on their journey, and those who had come before.

He looked to the Magi who stood beside him.

"And what now?" the Arimathean said.

"The peace will not be long," Balthazar said. "The Christ's power will not be held in human form. He will ascend before long."

Balthazar looked to the tomb.

"The Revelator has made sure all of the artifacts have been secreted away," Balthazar said. "The grail, the nails, the shroud. He will locate the spear and the others. All must be aligned for the Christ's return. The stars say two millennia hence. He will give you the maps, the locations of all."

"Why give them to me?" the Arimathean said.

"Who else?" Balthazar said. "I will return to S'iam B'ala. You will be the last. The last Magi on this earth. You, and your descendants, will be the guardians."

The two of them looked away, off into the horizon. Silent.

Both knew their minds were on their former companions.

The ones who had fallen on this quest.

"Was it worth it, Balthazar?" the Arimathean said. "All the death, the loss, the scars that remain unhealed?"

"It was. And it will be."

"And how do you know?"

"Faith."

A soft smile crossed Balthazar's face and his eyes shined silver and for a moment, the Arimathean felt a strange calm, a cool breeze about them.

He watched as the disciples marched off joyfully following the Christ, filled with a new fire, one which he could not help but feel.

Perhaps it was optimism.

Perhaps it was folly.

Perhaps, it was faith.

Faith found.

Or perhaps renewed.

He had seen much to instill and ignite that faith in this man, the Christ, over the years.

More than mere power, more than even the power over death he had just seen.

But the power of life.

The power of faith.

The power to not only present that to others, but to instill it in them, and perhaps, slowly, but surely, change the world through these people.

People like him, the Arimathean thought.

For if he could believe, if he could change, if he could gain his faith, then there may be hope for anyone.

So he watched as the procession continued, as people began to gather about them in the distance, as slowly, a new day was dawning.

He watched Magdalene ahead of him.

Smiled.

And he readied himself to join her.

Expecting Balthazar to do the same.

However, he did not.

The rasping sound of strained breathing caused the Arimathean to turn, and when he did, he saw Balthazar fall to the ground, clutching his chest, falling on his back, his eyes to the heavens.

A strange smile danced along the Magi's lips and his head shook back and forth slightly.

"I… should have known…" Balthazar gasped.

The Arimathean was at his side immediately, kneeling over him, frantic.

"What can I do? Balthazar! What is happening?"

"I… am…" Balthazar gasped. "The Christ will only survive on this world for another 40 days at most, he cannot continue, his spirit is too tethered to the heavens, his body cannot sustain it. I… am now the same way… I have spent too much time in the nether realms… and when the Christ saved me, he could only do so by connecting my soul to his consciousness… but… I have not the power… my body is not as powerful, anywhere near as powerful as his… I cannot sustain it…"

"So what can we do? What can I do?" the Arimathean placed his hands on Balthazar's shoulders and watched as his face, still smiling, grew dim, his eyes glowing silver all the more. "Is there a spell or a charm or something I can do? Something?"

"No, my friend, this is how it has to be, for now," Balthazar said, looking him in the face. "You… are the one he has chosen… you… are the one who will walk this earth until he returns again… and when he does… you… you… will see me once more… then, you will know his time is nigh…"

"What do you mean, I will walk this earth until he returns?" the Arimathean said.

"You… will not die, you cannot die," Balthazar said, "until the Christ's next arrival on this earth…you are the guardian…"

"But how? Why me?" the Arimathean said. "What about Magdalene, or the Revelator, or Simon Peter, or you?"

"You are the one he has chosen… and he has done so in great wisdom…" Balthazar said, lifting his hand up to touch the face of the Arimathean, and smiling as his amethyst eyes returned to him and then, slowly, were engulfed by the silver waves again. "Goodbye, my friend… I will see you… again…"

And then, Balthazar faded away, his body drained, his hand fallen to the earth.

But still, the smile remained on his face, his eyes, glowed silver intensely and then, then, they returned to their darkened hue, as they were when he was first born of the earth, many centuries earlier.

The Arimathean stayed kneeling beside his fallen friend, overwhelmed with waves of emotion that churned within him, sadness and uncertainty, eclipsing the joy he had dared to feel not a moment before upon the return of the Christ.

He watched as the Christ and his followers faded into the distance, saw Magdalene's form, dark and lithe, join them into mirage and then, nothing.

Nothing but earth and sky before him.

He looked down to Balthazar's body, but in an instant it too was gone, in a flash of light that burned white hot without a sound and soared to the heavens, leaving nothing of him behind.

Nothing but his words.

His words.

Which echoed, still, in the Arimathean's mind.

"You… are the one he has chosen… you… are the one who will walk this earth until he returns again… and when he does… you… you… will see me once more… then, you will know his time is nigh… you… will not die, you cannot die… until the Christ's next arrival on this earth…you are the guardian…"

The Arimathean let the earth pass through his hands, let the dust scatter to the wind, and lifted himself from the ground, to stand tall amidst the world around him.

He looked to the sky, cloudless and clear and blue, a blank slate.

And then to the earth before him, desolate and forbidding, devoid of another soul.

He felt a cool breeze once more.

Heard little more than silence.

And stranded there, between heaven and earth, he felt very much alone.

FORTY-SIX

With deadly silence and precision, the arrows rained down upon the centurions, cutting them down and clearing the entranceway to the palace.

Once within, he was one with the shadows, emerging with quick blades to slice the throats of all guards before words could escape, warning their brethren.

Or warning his true prey.

Before long, more than three dozen guards lie dead, their blood staining the marble floors, marking the trail to a room which had already seen its generous share of blood drained over the past several years.

The throne room.

The sacrifice pit.

The home of the king.

And now, the bejeweled, diabolical womb of the evil of Tiberius.

The warrior entered the room with stealth, expecting resistance, but, surprisingly, finding none.

Out of the corner of his eye, he saw the frightened, whimpering figure of Pilate scurry like a rat, towards a pillar. The warrior hurtled a knife Pilate's way, missing the Roman governor and embedding in the wall.

And as he saw the blade stick, he felt another blade soar past his own head, just missing.

He turned, just in time, to see the armored, muscled body of the Roman emperor, Tiberius, broadsword in hand, hacking down at him.

He dodged the emperor's blow just in time, doffed his cloak and threw it up at the emperor to distract him and with an enchantment it turned to mist, and through it, the warrior fired a handful of shuriken, and listened as they found their way into the emperor's flesh.

With a wave of his hand, he dismissed the fog and saw the Roman lying bleeding on the floor, all six of the shuriken embedded in his body.

The warrior bounded to the body of Tiberius, and raised his sword.

The emperor looked up at him and smiled.

"Barabbas…" the emperor said, through blood-speckled teeth.

"Look upon the face of your conqueror, and bid farewell to your life, and the end of Roman rape of our lands!" Barabbas said, and he thrust the sword downward, again, and again, into the body of Tiberius, until he felt not only satisfied in the death of his enemy, but the exorcism of his own ghosts, his own hatred of Rome, and the rulers who had oppressed him, and his people.

And when the body of Tiberius was still, mangled and bleeding, Barabbas stepped away.

He turned, and looked to where Pilate was hidden.

"Pilate! Come hither, and live, or make me find you, and die," Barabbas said.

Pilate emerged, slowly, his hands up, his brow and face slick with sweat and fear.

Barabbas stepped towards him, pointed his sword at him, as Pilate stood mere feet away, still unarmed, still sobbing with surrender.

"You know me, you have seen what I can do," Barabbas said. "You have seen me kill an emperor, and other far greater men than you. So know this: That your life is now and will forever be, in my hands. And while I will be merciful now, if you are not just in your ways with my people, if you are not just in your life, or your treatment of the followers of the Christ, your life will be forfeit to me. I will find you. I will hunt you down. And your life will be…"

But the final words never came, they remained caught in his throat, mingled with blood, coughed forth from the mouth of Barabbas, as he felt one dagger go in, deep and deadly, into his back, and then another, and another.

Barabbas reached behind him to pull the steel from him, threw it to the ground, but it was too late, the damage was done, and Barabbas fell to the palace floor as his life drained red from him.

As standing over him, was the mangled body of Tiberius, no longer dead, but reanimated by the power of the demon still holding throne over its soul.

Satan.

A snide, serpentine smile danced over the demon-human symbiote's face as he drew closer, circling Barabbas, his fingers steepled in malevolent contemplation.

"Barabbas, Barabbas, Barabbas… what shall I do with you? What shall I do with your body when you are no more?"

He kneeled over the heaving, coughing body, whispering.

"I have so little time to decide, for your death is so near," the Roman purred, putting the back of his hand to Barabbas' cheek as the dying man attempted to lurch away.

"You… will never… defeat…" Barabbas coughed. "This fire… will live…on for eternity…"

The Roman gently smiled, shook his head, and rubbed a wound on his shoulder.

"So close, Barabbas, so close, but not enough," he said. "Just like your movement, just like the Christ, who will soon leave you all behind."

"His body... like mine... may leave this earth, but his spirit, my spirit, will live on..." Barabbas said, defiant to the end.

"Oh Barabbas," the Tiberius-Satan symbiote said, kneeling over Barabbas' body. "You should've just quit while you were ahead."

Barabbas' eyes opened with a violent explosion, his teeth gritted, every fibre of his being in agony, fighting through the pain with his last fading spark, he grabbed the knife from the ground next to him and in one lightning move, his aim was true.

He thrust the blade deep into the neck of the Roman, into his jugular, and Tiberius' body froze, then collapsed to the floor. The emperor's blood spilled upon the cold marble, upon the knife, and upon Barabbas, who smiled one last time before his blade arm fell.

And their twin pools of blood grew in hatred and fire, commingling and draining as a stream across the ground, in a violent path.

"My God…" Barabbas said, smiling. "…into your hands I command my spirit."

And then, he was gone.

The room was silent.

The bodies still.

Pilate peered about them, uncertain, unknowing, what to do next.

And then, the bleeding, mangled, Satan-possessed body of the emperor rose up, reanimated, and smiled sardonically.

"Oh… my god," Pilate gasped.

"No… wrong guess…" the Tiberius-Satan symbiote smirked.

"How…" Pilate said.

"My power… the residual power of the sacrifices, the blood… is still allowing me to remain here…" the demon-human growled, before grimacing, as he grasped at his chest in pain.

"But the risen Christ, his power, is too much…merely being upon this earth, already I feel my hold upon this world, this body, slipping from me," Satan hissed through Tiberius' bloody lips.

"Then we are doomed?" Pilate said.

"No," Satan said. "His energy is powerful, but too powerful for this earthen realm. He cannot remain here for more than 40 days before he will ascend to the higher realm. During

that time his ways will reign upon this earth and his followers
will be protected and immune from our attacks. For a short time
after as well, as he will no doubt imbue them with his Holy Spirit
and power. But they were not born to it, they cannot sustain it, as
he would, and so they will eventually become vulnerable, and
when they do, when their spiritual fires have retreated into their
bodies, we will unleash suffering upon them like the world has
never known!"

"But what of the followers they gather?" Pilate said.
"Surely before the Christ leaves, he and his disciples will
perform great deeds of power, and they will amass a mighty
army of converts."

"They will," the Satan-Tiberius symbiote said. "But like
the disciples, they too can and will be slain, in public and
perverse fashion. And when enough have been humiliated and
destroyed, those sheep who have chosen to follow will find
themselves too fearful to do so. They may believe, but they will
not dare share it, not in a public place."

"But what of those who chronicle these times, these
people, these events?" Pilate said.

The demon-human cackled.

"Pilate, you are most ignorant," he said. "That is the
easiest to control. That which is written can be rewritten,

destroyed or lost to time, especially when those in power control the means of dissemination of the words.

"The people will believe what is written, and if we are the writers and the gateways to the words, we will control that which is in their hearts and minds."

Pilate smirked.

"When the Christ has ascended to heaven and his followers destroyed," Satan-Tiberius said, "he will not be able to return to his earth in human form for almost two millennia. So it has been written in the stars by his own God. It will be upon the people of this world to sustain his presence and vibration. And as we have both seen and experienced to our enjoyment, they are weak, stupid and easily swayed to selfishness and evil."

The body of Tiberius began to emit a foul, sulphuric stench and a fetid smoke began to slither from its pores. The symbiote coughed and blood splattered from the body's maw.

"We may not have succeeded in bringing a literal hell to this accursed planet, but we can damn it to a figurative one and bring it an untold misery by the hands and blackened hearts of its own people."

Pilate, satisfied, filled a goblet with wine and drank deeply.

"This body is not long for me," the demon-human rasped. "Fortunately, I have another quick at hand, which will prove to be a most magnificent instrument for my evil."

The Tiberius-Satan symbiote gazed darkly upon Pilate and the latter's veins ran cold.

The symbiote laughed.

"Not you, Pilate, you pathetic cur," he said. "I have a far more glorious and sinister throne in mind."

And at that, as the growled words hung in the air, borne aloft by the stench of death and dementia emanating from the collapsing body of Tiberius, the palace doors were hurled open and the crash echoed through the halls with a shock.

A sharp, pale, sliver of a man entered, oozing a sardonic poison in every mannerism and movement as he sneered upon the temple's trappings and Pilate's stunned face.

The man bore the robes of Roman royalty, and shimmering armor untouched by battle. Upon his head, haloing a rat-like face and cold, cavernous eyes, was a golden bough of gilded leaves and glittering gems. Perched upon his shoulder was the messenger, the jet black raven that had brought him forth to this place he spat upon as beneath anything but his contempt, beneath any use but as a gateway to power, to a throne he would soon claim as he ascended to rule the Empire.

And the throne he would become, the human host, for Satan's reign on earth.

The knife of a man sliced through the room with malice, past Pilate, and leered at the fading body of Tiberius.

"You summoned me?" the man smirked, spitting through gritted teeth, "my lord."

"Yes, I did… I have… use for you…" Satan said, as the head of Tiberius raised and he met the new man's eyes and a fire burned, as an unholy energy passed between them and Satan joyfully claimed his new host.

There was a dark cloud laced with crimson light that stabbed into the new host, permeating the room with a despicable stench, as the old body of Tiberius collapsed to the ground, a used, useless, tattered marionette of battered flesh and bone.

The fresh host of Satan stood tall, its eyes alight in deep crimson, its mouth curved with shark teeth in a horrible smile.

He stood tall.

A new host of Satan.

A new Emperor of Rome.

An old evil, reborn.

"Yes…" Satan hissed through new lips, "you shall be a fine throne for me, a fine throne indeed… Emperor… Caligula."

FORTY-SEVEN: EPILOGUE

The wooden raft crawled to the island's edge in the heart of the night. Its sole occupant's torch sliced the darkness, the fire's crackling breaking the constant sound of waves, lapping around the man leaving the murky depths behind.

He was clad in thick black robes, layers, the innermost doused in medicinal oils and salves. Glistening silver bracelets about his neck and wrists were carved in holy sigils.

His muscles ached as he pulled the boat ashore on the island, hiding it amidst the trees. He hurled a loaded satchel around him as he moved slowly, painfully towards the island's interior. One hand was closed around the pack slung around him, the other on the heavy chunk of wood burning bravely before him.

His body was a rude temple of pain, scarred and burned, shambling through the brush, under the vast expanse of stars.

His wounds still had not healed.

He had been burned alive.

Boiled.

His skin was still pestilent. Even with his advanced healing abilities and the mystical properties of chants and salves, the wounds had practically destroyed him.

His body shook as he fell to the ground. He convulsed, his body quaking against the rocks and dirt. His eyes went clear and white and the visions came, again, quickly at first and then, slower, slower, slower, until his body began to calm, almost as if adjusting to the power it was being forced to wield.

He caught himself, regained his focus.

He continued forward, towards his refuge.

He thought back.

It had not been long.

Not been long after the ascension of the Christ, after the Arimathean and Magdalene had gone into exile, disappearing to Merovingea, after the word began to spread, as the number of disciples began to grow.

It began slowly, at first. A few disappearances. A few of the louder followers, those most openly calling for revolution. Those fanning a rebellion of the more tangible means rather than the spiritual means espoused by the Christ.

At first they disappeared in the night, and rumors spread, of the presence, growing. The eye, upon them.

But it failed to diminish them, failed to stunt their growth, their passion. If anything, it made them more determined, more obdurate, more rebellious.

And so, soon, the pretense was gone.

And so, quickly, Rome arrived, not in a splendid array of vehicles, but in a spiked glove, crushing them in its grasp. The sadistic claws of its leader.

Caligula.

Soon there was no secret to the penalty for belief.

It was death.

First torture.

Then death.

Most public, served for the masses, both as warning and entertainment.

But still, the movement grew.

And so, the Romans became all the more determined to eliminate those at its forefront.

It was easy for most. They were orators, not warriors, and words were no match for steel.

But those such as the disciples, such as him, such as John the Revelator, became far more difficult to find, and destroy.

Finally captured through the herculean efforts of scores of warriors and the dark magicks of two seers, he was finally enchained, imprisoned, and brought before the arena.

But he refused to die, and could not be defeated. And the Romans, fearing the power of a champion displayed before the people as able to defeat the arena's greatest dooms, put forth rumor of a secret ignominious death of the Revelator and removed him from the arena's competition.

Ensnared again through blackest Satanic sorcery, he was removed to the private torture chambers of Caligula and his enclave, kept at bay through ancient spells and mighty charms. There he was slowly subjected to a perverse chain of slow destruction, until Caligula bored of him, and ordered him destroyed, boiled in oil, "anointed in pain," as the sadistic emperor put it.

But still, he survived and, left for dead, with his last reserve of strength and power, was able to escape.

But he knew it would not be for long, so he quickly packed his means for healing, his sacred scrolls, his only pathways to survival physically and spiritually and he left, to remain in exile, for as long as needed.

His only means of communication, of connection, with the world, his lifeline, was the white owl hovering above him.

Seraphim. The familiar of the Magi. Which accompanied him to the island upon which he now landed.

The island of Patmos.

Perhaps it had been the pain, the torture endured, perhaps something else, but from the journey's onset, he had felt something, something in his mind, something like an eggshell, slowly cracking, at the base of his skull, slowly breaking open to reveal…

Something.

What, he wasn't sure.

But something.

Something he felt taking over, taking over his mind.

And as the moon lingered overhead, and he looked up to its light, the last embers of his torch flickered out, leaving him in darkness, with only the beacon of that orb and the stars scattered about it, to guide him, as the shadow of the lone owl soaring above cast a dark shape within it.

He continued on, guided by instinct more than anything to the edge of the cave, the place he had visited once before, long ago, that lingered along the periphery of his mind.

And then… it started.

Slowly at first.

Then in rapid chaos.

His body began to shake, to convulse, as his vision blurred, and his mind began to race.

Within his mind, images exploded in a frenzy, tearing through his brain. They were like nothing he had seen before.

Horrible and terrific.

Astounding and insane.

He felt his body savagely lurching. It was no longer of his control. His mind filled with fear as he felt himself pushed by unknown forces quickly and powerfully, over the rocks and dirt and into the cave, where he flew into convulsions. His body tossed to the ground, his mind exploding, overwhelmed, his voice a guttural torrent of strange and unknown language, a hurricane of thought and movement and sound that crashed and erupted, until finally dying, dying down, his mind suddenly still, his body suddenly healed, his essence immersed in calm, cold and entirely clear.

His mind became a brilliant white.

A blank page.

And then, with deliberate, silent precision, his slowly sat and from his bag removed a scroll and pen.

Once he had regained himself, he righted his body and clutched the papers and the quill and, still sweating and frantic, he began to write, feverishly, what he had just been shown, been told, what had just raced through his brain.

His mind became a peaceful blue flame. He saw words emblazoned in gold upon the scroll of his brain, and putting his hand to the tablet before him, he wrote…

Wrote…

"Look, he is coming with the clouds, and every eye will see him, even those who pierced him; and all the peoples of the earth will mourn because of him. So shall it be…"

To be continued in

Book Three Of

The Arimathean Trilogy...

DisIntegration

THE ARIMATHEAN TRILOGY

BOOK ONE: THE ARIMATHEAN

BOOK TWO: THE BLOOD OF DESTINY

BOOK THREE: DISINTEGRATION

Question and Answer with author Sean Leary

By Connie Corcoran Wilson

Sean Leary has had an eclectic career as a writer, beginning with his first published stories at age 11 in the national newspaper The Comics Buyers Guide. Since then, he has written for scores of newspapers, magazines, websites and blogs. He's written for the theater, television and films, and he's had over two dozen books published.

However, until recently, Leary had never written a novel. His 2012 debut in that arena, *The Arimathean*, was as unexpected as it was unique. Whereas Leary's previous works resembled the quirky humor of David Sedaris and Dave Barry or the spiritual and humanistic styles of John Steinbeck and Nick Hornby, *The Arimathean* and its follow-up, *The Blood of Destiny*, released in 2014, are action-adventure tales steeped in speculative historical fiction.

The Arimathean asked the question 'What if the three Magi and Joseph of Arimathea were ninja wizards sent to protect Jesus, Mary and Joseph from the evil devices of Satan and King Herod?' The book went on to answer the question, veering from a roller coaster of popcorn movie fun to a thought-provoking meditation on faith.

The follow-up book, *The Blood of Destiny*, has posed the question 'What if the disciples were ninjas fighting to prevent Satan from turning Jesus' body into a zombie Antichrist?' Again, Leary has taken what on the surface appears a slam-bang popcorn movie premise and imbued it with surprising depth, introspection and spirituality.

Leary recently took time out to answer a few questions about *The Arimathean, The Blood of Destiny* and his other works.

Arimathean Question and Answer:

Q: *The Arimathean* begins with a very unique premise. Where did you get the idea?

A: It actually goes back to my childhood. Having been raised Catholic, my household, during the Christmas season, was always decorated with a Nativity scene. For those unfamiliar with Catholicism, a Nativity scene is a diorama of the birth of Christ. It features a small shack or barn-like structure, and, a manger, where the holy family settled in Bethlehem for the birth of the baby Jesus. It also features a number of modest sized statues, figurines, representing the characters involved in the story.

The figurines are typically plaster or plastic---my family had both, the plaster, which was broken within a few years yielding to a plastic set that lasted much longer – but they featured the same cast of characters: a Joseph, a Mary, a Jesus, a few farm animals, usually a mule and some sheep, and maybe a few camels. Then there would be the handful of shepherds and the angel. And, of course, the three wise men, also known as the three kings or the three Magi.

The figurines, at least in my house, were typically of a size between that of a 'Star Wars' action figure and a Mego Marvel SuperHeroes action figure. As a young boy, I had a decent array of action figures. And, being a young boy, I would come up with various battle scenarios for them. When Christmastime arrived and the Nativity set was unpacked and displayed, I didn't necessarily regard it with the utmost sacrosanct respect that my parents would have liked. Instead, I saw it as an opportunity to add a few new characters to my own mix of imaginary battles.

As such, amidst the 'Star Wars' figures, 'G.I. Joe' guys, Marvel SuperHeroes, Micronauts and other action figures of the time, various Nativity figures would take their place in strange battles I would envision and act out on a daily basis. Luke Skywalker, Spider-Man and Time Traveler would stand beside the three Magi battling against Darth Vader, Baron Karza and the ninja agents of COBRA as they strove to protect or abduct the holy family. I know some thought these war games blasphemous. I found them to be terrific fun. I would venture to guess most pre-teen and elementary school boys – as I was at the time – would agree with me.

As I got older and discovered girls --- and likewise discovered girls weren't impressed by boys who played with action figures, let alone played with Nativity set figurines pretending to be action figures--- I abandoned my war games. But I never forgot them.

Tales of these strange bastardizations of pop culture and Biblical storytelling would come up in conversations with my family over hams and pumpkin pies around the holiday season. Sometimes, this was to embarrass me in front of whatever girl I was dating at the time. But most of the time, it was just good fun. I reminisce today on the goofy and strange things I did when I was a kid.

It was back in the late-1990s, after a particularly fun and nostalgic Christmas season at home that I got the idea for what would become *The Arimathean*. I was driving home, the two to three hour trek over snowy highways, and my mind began to wander, thinking of the games of my youth, which we had just laughed over minutes earlier, and I began to formulate a story, a really interesting action tale, in which the Nativity scenes I'd envisioned came to life. What if the Magi were warriors sent to protect the holy family? What if they were knights, or soldiers, or, maybe even ninja wizards? I was so excited by it, I ended up pulling over and writing it down, jotting down all the ideas I had. But I didn't really have to worry about forgetting the idea, because I really loved it.

Q: That was back in the late-1990s. *The Arimathean* as a novel wasn't finished until 2012. What took you so long to complete the novel? Why did you decide to wait?

A: Well, as with most writers and creative people, I have a ton of ideas, and they sort of gestate until one of them demands to be brought to life. *The Arimathean* sort of sat on the backburner, tucked into my brain. From time to time, I would jot ideas for it down into my notebooks. I remember telling my friend and fellow author, Matthew Clemens, about the idea in '99 or so, when we were doing signings for a jam book we collaborated on. He thought it was a great idea. Every time we'd get together he would encourage me to write the darn thing.

Around 2001 I started writing it, chapter by chapter. Over the next eight years it was put together a chapter at a time, in dribs and drabs, always in the background as I was devoting the majority of my time to other projects. In 2009 I started working on it with greater urgency. In the fall of 2011 I began devoting even more time to it. I finished up the first very rough draft in February 2012, a better draft in March 2012, and started polishing it into a final draft during the spring and summer of 2012. From spring to fall 2012, I worked relentlessly on the novel. Every spare moment I got, apart from my substantial time devoted to being a stay-at-home father and an education student getting my masters from the University of Southern California or working to pay the bills was dedicated to *The Arimathean*. I didn't go out on the weekends. I didn't party. I didn't sit around and watch TV when my son was asleep. I worked on my novel. In mid-September 2012 I finally got to the point where I knew it was complete.

Q: You mention Matthew Clemens, who has written a number of books and is a frequent collaborator with Max Allan Collins. The two are best known for their crime fiction works and novelizations of TV shows like "CSI" and "Dark Angel." How did Matthew become involved?

A: Matthew and I have been friends since the late-'90s and I've always had a terrific amount of respect for him and his talents. He had known about the idea for quite some time. As I said previously, I told him about it back when Clinton was in the White House. He encouraged me to pursue it, feeling it had a lot of potential. Once I started really getting into it, I asked him if he would be so kind as to take a look at the book as I was putting chapters together and as I got a first draft completed. He provided some great advice and a much needed second pair of eyes belonging to someone who is well versed in the craft. His wife, Pam, also read that evolving first draft and provided some terrific advice. As a writer, it's always important to have another reader or two, whether an editor or a friend, because you become so immersed in the work that it's difficult for you to be objective. You lose perspective. Matthew and Pam were excellent beta readers, and I'm very, very grateful to them for all their insight and support along the way. And they're just terrific people. I'm blessed to have them in my life.

Q: What other books or authors influenced you while working on *The Arimathean*?

A: Growing up, there were a number of books that informed my experience as a writer and reader. Having grown up Catholic, one was the Bible. Growing up a geek and fantasy-adventure fan, other significant books, for me, were J.R.R. Tolkien's 'The Lord of the Rings' novels. Others were C.S. Lewis' books and the works of fantasy authors like Michael Moorcock, Edgar Rice Burroughs and Ray Bradbury.

All of them appealed to my nascent imagination with fantastic tales of good versus evil, of amazing creatures and tremendous battles, and of faith winning out against an unrelenting darkness. All of them inform and influence *The*

Arimethean, and the stories which will follow in the upcoming

books rounding out *The Arimathean trilogy*.

All of the books, from this first volume to the third, are

meant to be the type that the younger me would've devoured

again and again. I've written them in the hope that other readers

will enjoy them the same way.

Q: The characters within the book are Biblically based.

You take some liberties with their stories. How much research

on the Biblical characters did you do for the book? How much

of it is just the product of your imagination?

A: I did do some research, but I didn't base a lot of the

book on it. I read the four gospels several times and read the

whole of the New Testament twice. So I had a feeling for how to

write the book and how to trace the storyline. But it's obvious

that I did make a lot of it up. The Magi are only mentioned in

one book, the gospel of Matthew, and that's essentially a cameo

appearance. Joseph of Arimathea is mentioned in all the gospels,

but it's really only in the context of him giving his tomb to Jesus

after Christ's death. So there's a lot of leeway taken with those

characters. As for the other characters that pop up in the book,

again, I had to take a lot of liberties in fleshing them out and

making them more complex. I tended to incorporate characters I

felt fit the story, as well as those I have always found fascinating, going back to my early years in Catholic school. The Magi, Joseph of Arimathea, John the Revelator, Mary Magdalene, they're all characters I have found to be intriguing in a variety of ways. And then there are characters like the Watchers, the Elohim, who are mentioned in the Old Testament, that I have always found fascinating, so I decided to incorporate them as well.

Q: How did you handle Joseph and Mary? Isn't it a slippery slope you're walking, writing them as real people, as human beings with feelings and concerns that are realistic given the situations, while trying not to offend any believers?.

A: I was raised Catholic, and I still consider myself a Christian and a faithful believer in God. I wrote the characters with a lot of respect for them and consideration for how they were portrayed. I based a lot of their characteristics on the writings in the Bible. I tried to write from their perspectives in regard to what they went through, and the things I made up, the dialogue I made up, was all with due respect and portrays them as good, moral people. A lot of their characteristics to paint them as complex characters are based upon the gospels. I figured that every child, even Jesus, is influenced by his parents and by the way they're raised. So I took certain details from Jesus' sermons and parables and extrapolated them and applied them to form the backstories of Mary and Joseph. That way, it honors the Biblical material and also makes sense from a familial perspective. I'm not out to offend anyone. I'm trying to tell a story that is entertaining to read from a fantasy and adventure perspective and has a moral core to it that resonates as an echo of its source material and resonates with believers today as well. This is really no different than someone making a film like "Jesus of Nazareth" or "The Passion of the Christ" or "Jesus Christ Superstar." The source material is reflected, but you also have to take liberties along the way in making up dialogue or adding scenes or actions to tell a fuller story.

Q: How is your own religious background reflected?

A: I went to Catholic elementary and junior high schools, a Catholic high school and a Catholic university through my first year of college before I transferred to a state university. I lapsed from the Catholic Church, but never abandoned my belief in Christ and certainly not my faith in God. That's where I remain today. I attend a variety of Christian churches because I believe they each have different things to offer. I can't say I adhere to a specific branch of religious faith, but I believe in the basic tenets involved, the golden rule of loving God and loving one another that Christ espoused. And, even through all the ninjas and such in the book, you see that faith reflected.

Q: How is faith reflected?

A: The Arimathean, the character, is really an allegory for humanity and man's struggle with faith. The characters within the book represent different belief structures. Their dialogue reflects that. The Arimathean himself asks a lot of tough questions that I think almost everyone has asked in regard to God's place on earth and in their lives and in the role of humanity. Balthazar represents faith. His answers realistically reflect the answers I often got in Catholic school when I would ask the priests and teachers similar questions.

Q: How much research did you do regarding the time period? Is the book a realistic portrayal of the era?

A: Not much historical research beyond the re-examination of the Bible. It's not what I would call a painstakingly realistic representation of the historical period. I began to research it, but the more I did, the more I came across things that didn't serve the story well, so I decided to eliminate the minute details and instead paint with broad strokes to capture a feel for the time. It feels like a Biblical epic. It has the details we've come to expect from Biblical stories, whether in films or on TV. I was more concerned with just telling a really compelling story on a number of levels and less concerned with things like whether or not they would've realistically been riding horses or camels or walking on foot. Horses just fit the story best, so they're on horses. If the characters are traveling a long distance and being attacked by demons and Roman centurions, it made more sense to me to have them on horses rather than on foot. If you want to read a breathtakingly researched, photo-realistic look at the time period, look elsewhere. If you want to read a fun action story with ninjas and demons and magic and monsters that also has some intriguing and thought-provoking dialogue, this is the book for you.

Q: The book has some particularly violent and gory sequences. Other sequences are quite beautiful and uplifting. What led you to emphasize the violence?

A: To create tension. To create a sense of fear, a sense of danger. Think about it: Almost every reader is going to come into this book knowing the end of the story. The challenge for me was to create suspense and tension in a story where you already know the ending. So I have to really ramp up the evil they face, really ramp up the obstacles and the opposition. I needed to get readers to the point where I create enough tension and suspense that they might actually ask themselves, 'If he's changing things up this much, is he going to change the ending? Is he actually going to kill off one of these characters or do something really crazy at the end?' At the very least, I just wanted readers to have fun reading the story, and to create that roller coaster you need to have really powerful and strong heroes and maybe even stronger villains and great opposition for those heroes to overcome. That's what creates the tension and gets people hooked. That's what keeps people reading.

Q: The book is very cinematic. Do you see it as a movie?

A: The way I typically write stories, whether as part of a novel or short stories, is I envision them in my head as movies. I try to describe what I'm seeing in my head for the reader. So, yeah, of course I see *The Arimathean* as a film. And, yeah, of course, like a lot of authors, I would love to see my book as a movie. I know some books don't work as films, but action and fantasy translates particularly well to the big screen, especially when you're dealing with otherworldly powers and creatures and a broader canvas. I think *The Arimathean trilogy* would make a terrific set of films. Or, at least, they make a great set of films in my imagination, as I'm seeing them in my head.

Q: If, as you say, you see the story as a film in your head as you're writing it, what actors would you cast?

A: Really there were only two that I recognized, to be honest. For example, the Joseph and Mary in my head, the Balthazar in my head, were people that I have never seen before. So they're actors in the theater company of my own imagination. One I would cast is Dwayne Johnson, the Rock, as Gaspar. He just has the right presence and look to be Gaspar, and he's got the action star background. I think he'd be great casting in that part. The other is Hugh Jackman as The Arimathean. I think Hugh Jackman is a phenomenal actor. He would be perfect for the title role in all three movies. But, you know, that's sort of a pipe dream at this point, wishful thinking!

Q: What do you see the future holding for *The Arimathean*? You mention it's the first in a trilogy, how is the trilogy going to play out?

A: When I first got the idea, it was for a massive novel that began with the birth of Christ and ended far in the future with the second coming and the apocalypse. It's basically following the story of the New Testament – it begins with the birth of Christ in the gospels and ends with the end of the world in Revelation. As I began writing chapters and refining my thinking about it, it made the most sense to break it up into a trilogy. So that's what I've done. The first book, *The Arimathean*, takes place in the days just prior to and after the birth of Christ. The second book, which I'm writing right now, tentatively called *The Blood of Destiny,* takes place around the time of the death of Christ. And the third book, tentatively titled *DisIntegration*, takes place in the future, around 2033 and involves the apocalypse and the second coming.

So in essence, the first two books cover the gospels and the last book is Revelation. However, I take great liberties with all of them and tell very different stories while retaining the same general outlines. As for when the trilogy will be complete, I don't know. I'm writing the very rough draft of the second book right now. I have an outline and a few chapters of the third book. But they're far from being done. I don't have any set date to finish or any release dates for the second and third books in the trilogy. I'm going to write the best books I possibly can, tell the most entertaining and imaginative stories I can, and when I feel I've done my best, they'll be released. I can say that I'm extremely excited about being immersed in writing the trilogy and that, unlike the first book, the second and third won't take more than a decade to become reality. When all are done and released, I hope they form a terrific trilogy that pleases readers and keeps them coming back, again and again. And, at every turn, I hope they enjoy them. Really, that's what it's all about. I want people to enjoy reading the books. I want kids like me, book fans like I was as a kid, to love *The Arimathean trilogy* the same way I loved those C.S. Lewis and Tolkien and Burroughs books I read as a kid.

Q: Any last thoughts?

A: I just want to say thank you to anyone who bought the book, anyone who read it, and I hope they enjoyed it. In however small a way I hope it made their life better for having read it, even if just as entertainment. And if you did enjoy it, please tell your friends to check it out! I hope people enjoy the books, and I thank you for reading them.

Blood of Destiny Question and Answer:

After being released in November 2012, Sean Leary's *The Arimathean* became a best-seller over the course of the holiday season and into the next year. After graduating with honors from the Masters program at University of Southern California in December 2013, and during the Christmas season of 2013 and into the early months of 2014, he wrote and finished the second book of the Arimathean trilogy, *The Blood of Destiny*. He recently took time out to answer questions about this second book, and the upcoming third book in the trilogy, *DisIntegration*.

Q: You had mentioned earlier that the first book in the trilogy was written and rewritten in dribs and drabs over the course of almost a decade, from 2002-2012. The second book, however, was written in less than two months. What accounts for the difference in time?

A: The second book was really gestating in my head during the time I was finishing up The Arimathean in 2012. Obviously, when you look at that book, there are various ways in which I'm planting seeds for the second, just as there are various seeds planted in both books that will bloom in the third. So The Blood of Destiny was hovering about my imagination during that time. I started kind of scribbling notes down in the summer and fall of 2013 while I was finishing up grad school, but I didn't have the time to dedicate to it until I graduated from USC in December 2013. I sat down and started putting together an outline in December, collecting notes and such in December and January, and started writing in late January with a self-imposed deadline of March 20, the first day of spring. I finished the book two days early. Why was it such a quick write, as opposed to the first novel? Well, obviously, I knew what I was doing the second time around. I had done it once before and I had a better idea of how to do it. Also, this book just came very easy to me. I don't know why. The ideas were just there and I put them down on paper and there was very little editing. Very little. I went through the book four times after that initial rough draft and there are very few changes other than one or two minor things and a few typos that needed to be cleaned up. I don't know why that is, but I'm not complaining! I hope the third book arrives that way and is just as quick to write.

Q: The second book starts with a scene reminiscent of the opening of the first book. Was that intentional?

A: Yeah. The Arimathean is the main character in all of the stories, and so in many ways, the books are about his evolution along the path, or lack thereof, and I like the idea of starting off the books with similar situations or scenarios to show

how he has changed, or, not changed. The third book in the trilogy, *DisIntegration*, is going to start the same way, or a similar way. The other reasons are that I like, and I think the reader enjoys, starting off with an action sequence to get things going from the get go and that scene establishes the hero, his power, and the villains and gives an outline of the plot and setting right from the start. It's not a cold opening. It grabs you right from the start, and that's what I like, to write in a propulsive fashion.

Q: There's also a chapter in the second book that is basically word-for-word an echo of a chapter in the first book. Was that planned before you wrote the first book or was it something you thought of as you were putting the second book together?

A: Yeah, it's pretty much the same chapter word-for-word and yes, it was very much planned when I was writing the Arimathean. That's the whole reason that chapter is in the Arimathean, because it's kind of incongruous in a way in that book. You read that chapter in the first book and it makes you think that it's a prophetic dream Balthazar is having about their current journey, and it puts you on edge because it's sort of a creepy non-sequitor, and that's part of why I put it in the first book, to create that feeling, that tone. But the main reason is to tie the two books together and to show how the stories are all one, that the characters and the themes overlap and that some of these characters, particularly the more spiritually linked, like the Magi or Christ, or the Arimathean, are sort of out of time, they don't adhere to the regular passing of time as regular humans do. And so that chapter is meant to be a bit paranormal, a bit spiritual, to show how time has no meaning and that the characters are, in some ways, aware of, or given some peek into, their destinies, which gives them a different perspective on their lives. You'll see the same thing in the third book, *DisIntegration*. It's not going to be the same device, where a chapter repeats, but there will be certain scenes or allusions in the first two books that will make greater sense when you see how they fit into the bigger picture which is portrayed in *DisIntegration*.

Q: You mention the third book of the Arimathean trilogy, *DisIntegration*. How much of it have you written and when can readers expect to see it?

A: I haven't written much. I have written the very last scene, or, one of the very last scenes. And I've written part of the very first scene. I have the overall plot in my head, and a lot of details, but it's not mapped out yet. I'm not sure when I'll have it finished. Maybe Christmas 2014 or Easter 2015. But if it takes a while, it may not be until Christmas 2015. It's the last book so I want to make sure it's perfect. Plus, I've got some other literary adventures I'd like to pursue and a few of those definitely will arrive before book three, and one or two might arrive.

Q: What are those "literary adventures?"

A: Even before *The Blood of Destiny* was finished I started working on a children's book with my son and his kindergarten class, called *Nine Little Ninjas*. It's for beginning readers and it teaches them about reading and math. I'm also working on another book for beginning readers with my son, Jackson, which is going to be called *Baby Bird*. I've probably got about three or four books of poetry finished which are waiting to be published, but who knows when those are going to see print. My play, *My Life As A Freak Magnet*, is going to be published in summer of 2014 so I'm overseeing that. And I've got another novel I'm writing, an erotic romance, called *Speed of Sound*, that may be done by summer or early fall of 2014. I'm not sure about that one, we'll see. But the two children's books and the published version of my play are definitely going to be out in the next few months. And then after that, who knows? I might do *Speed of Sound* or I might jump into *DisIntegration*. It all depends on where inspiration leads me.

Q: Back to *The Blood of Destiny*, the character of Barabbas seems to be almost the flip side of the coin to Jesus. Was that something you invented or something that you found in research?

A: Mostly something I invented, inspired by research. Barabbas was painted in different ways in the different gospels, with some calling him a revolutionary and others a thief. I thought it would be cool to create him as a Robin Hood type of character. I also thought it would be interesting to have him reflect a more earth-bound view of the spiritual revolution led by Jesus, because that's always the flip side of religious work – providing spiritual sustenance but also helping people who need help with the material, whether it's food or clothing or shelter or other needs.

Q: In the opening chapter in the new book, you incorporate the Sodomites as villains. What was the motivation or symbolism behind that?

A: The motivation was pretty simple, I wanted to ramp up the tension and the sense of danger so in addition to having the Roman centurions present and ready to kill the Arimathean, I also added the Sodomites lurking about in a creepy way. It also adds a strange and devious mood to the setting. I made them the Sodomites because I figured most people knew the Biblical story of Sodom and Gomorrah, the twin cities of evil, and calling them the Gommorites didn't sound anywhere near as sinister. The symbolism, which not only pops up in that first chapter but throughout, is the split between the old ways and the new, the old testament and the new, and the dividing line that was drawn historically by Christ and the events detailed in the story.

Q: So was Joseph of Arimathea a member of the Sanhedrin?

A: It's really uncertain as to who Joseph of Arimathea truly was, which is why I chose him as the main character in this trilogy. He, like the Magi, are sort of blank slates that can be turned into anything for the purpose of creating the story and advancing the greater plotlines and overarching symbolism of the tale. Joseph of Arimathea turns up in all four gospels but he's only mentioned in a line or two and it's not in any great detail. And the Magi only turn up in the Gospel of Matthew, which is why I mention in this book that there are connections between Matthew and the Magi. But I leave them vague because I want people to kind of fill in the blanks with their own imaginations. In my research there was a piece I read that said that Joseph of Arimathea was actually a member of the Sanhedrin. But there were also pieces that said he was Jesus' uncle, and others that said he was a nobleman or a rich man who was a follower of Christ. It worked for me, and for the story, to have him be a member of the Sanhedrin. I thought it would be intriguing for a number of reasons. It's also alluded to in the story that he and Matthew were kind of spies that were infiltrating organizations from within to bring change about, which I put in there because

Matthew is often reported as a tax collector or a Roman government worker, and I thought it was a neat idea to paint those characters as being double-agents or spies for the rebellion against the Roman empire. It also plays into the last third of the trilogy to have the Arimathean adept at infiltrating larger organizations, and it will also play into potential future books aside from the trilogy.

Q: Will there be future Arimathean books aside from the trilogy?

A: Well, let's just say there's a reason I put about 2,000 years between book two and book three. That's all I'll say for now. Although there's some really interesting foreshadowing of what happens in the future in the last few chapters of *The Blood of Destiny*, especially if you read the passages about the Arimathean and Magdalene.

Q: Women's equality and really equality between all people seem to be large overarching themes in this book. Was that intentional, and why?

A: Yeah, it was definitely intentional, and was definitely something I wanted to spotlight in the book. I've always felt that was one of the great aspects of Jesus' teachings, that all were equal and that people are judged on the quality of their character and their courage and their faith, rather than who they were otherwise. Jesus embraced people of all types, whether it was in his teachings or his selection of disciples or his followers, and I wanted that to be a major theme in this book. I think too often we see religion mistakenly and misguidedly used to denigrate women or put them in their place, so to speak, and I think that's very wrong, which is one reason why I made Magdalene and Tanara such powerful characters. Another reason is that I wanted girls to have a powerful female character to look up to, someone virtuous and strong and powerful. Which, again, is another reason why I wrote Magdalene as I did, as a warrior who was mistakenly and bitterly labeled as a witch or a prostitute because she was a powerful female. When you research the scriptures, there are debates in some quarters over whether Magdalene was a prostitute or whether she was merely labeled as such because she was an independent woman or because she hadn't married or whatever, and I think there's enough gray area there that shows that unfortunately women of that era, or really any era, can be mislabeled because of their power or their independence. I wanted Magdalene to represent that, in the best way, which is why I wrote her as a hero, as someone strong and amazing and beautiful and virtuous.

Q: The chapter where Mary says goodbye to Jesus is especially heartbreaking.

A: Another goal of mine with these books, the first two parts of the trilogy, especially, is to really humanize the characters and the situations. I think too often people feel distant from these characters, from people like Mary, because they seem more standoffish and don't seem like you and me. And really, they were human beings, they had feelings. And if you had to see your son treated the way Jesus was treated, it would break your heart. Even if you had faith in what he was doing, even if you had faith you would see him again, see him rise from the dead, it would absolutely break your heart to see him treated that way. Especially unjustly. And I wanted to bring that home in that chapter, to show Mary's faith and love for her son, and also to show just how powerful that was under the most difficult of circumstances.

Q: Do you think you'll catch a lot of flak for making the disciples ninja warriors?

A: I hope not, I hope people recognize what I'm doing and actually read the books and see that I'm handing the characters In a really cool and respectful way, when you think about it. Honestly, I'm just kind of making them cool and more accessible to a younger audience, or a different audience, in a lot of ways. But even beyond that, I think if you look at it from a historical perspective, I'm not stepping too far out of the box, I'm just looking at the box differently. If you read the gospels, there are instances of the disciples pulling swords or wanting to go to battle – the most prominent, perhaps, being when one of the disciples cuts off the soldier's ear when the soldiers come to arrest Jesus in Gethsemane. Historically, the disciples would've been trained to defend themselves as most male youths of that time were, so they were warriors in a way. I've just amped that up to a different level. Plus, I loved the idea of the disciples being sort of like the Seven Samurai or the Magnificent Seven, this cadre of brilliant warriors hand-picked by Jesus not only for their virtue but for their skills as warriors. It's pretty cool. It's fun. And I wanted other people reading the books to feel that, to think of the disciples as cool rather than just these stodgy historical figures of marble who seem so distant from us.

Q: Have you gotten a lot of flak from Christians or non-Christians about the series?

A: A little from each, in different ways, obviously. But not a lot, and it hasn't been too bad, knock wood. I have friends of all different religions and I have friends who are atheists or agnostics. I respect their beliefs and I ask they respect mine. I always tell anyone who raises an issue to read the book first and then make up their minds because I think anyone who actually looks at the material will find themselves pleasantly surprised, and that goes for both sides of the debate.

Q: Speaking of different perspectives, there are times in the book in which you seem to contradict yourself, or contradict the story, or tell it from different perspectives. Is this because you're reflecting that the characters don't know everything that's going on, or is it due to another literary device?

A: Yes to all. There are a lot of instances of uncertainty and secrecy amongst the characters. For example, Herod Antipas is trying to deceive the Roman hierarchy, Pilate is trying to deceive Herod Antipas and Tiberius is basically deceiving them both. Balthazar keeps secrets to himself, apart from anyone else. And the Arimathean isn't exactly the most forthcoming of characters in regard to his motivations. So, yes, I'm trying to reflect the different perspectives of each character, and if the characters aren't aware of the motivations or knowledge of the others, then I can't reflect that. And, to answer your other question, yes, it's actually kind of an homage to the four gospels, which reflect four different perspectives on the same story, the life and death of Christ. It's intriguing to me that you've got this canon that so many people take literally and just by sheer logic you cannot take it literally because literally you have four different versions of the exact same story within the same book, the Bible. I mean, which gospel do you take literally when they contradict each other and tell the same story differently? It just shows that every story is different in the eye of the beholder. You can have the same essential truths, but the interpretations and the perspectives offered are entirely subjective depending on the narrator's point of view. And that's also kind of one of the overarching themes of this trilogy, of this series, that sometimes what is important is the overarching message, the moral, that's being conveyed in the story, and that the stories themselves are edited and changed according to the narrator, according to the editor and according to the times. In these times, when zombies and ninjas and demons and superheroes are the elements that captivate people, why shouldn't I spin parables that incorporate these elements in order to get people's attention and try to captivate an audience into possibly absorbing a really positive story with a good moral center? It's funny, that's one of the things I've debated with people who have charged me with being heretical or with contradicting the word of God – who are they to say how God's word is conveyed? Doesn't it reflect a strange lack of esteem to think that God stopped speaking to us two thousand years ago? That God stopped selecting messengers of his word more than two millennia ago? Who's to say that it isn't God who is inspiring me to write these stories, to bring his word to a new generation, in a way that's much more captivating and entertaining to them, in a way that they'll understand and find more accessible? After all, wouldn't you rather have someone creating something like this, of positive value, trying to bring across positive morals and a positive message, rather than something that's disposable and nihilistic? I guess in some ways it's a mirror. Your reaction to it reflects your own perception and your own values.

Q: So, signing off, what can you tell us about the third book, *DisIntegration*?

A: I don't want to reveal too much or spoil anything, but obviously, if you've read *The Blood of Destiny* and *The Arimathean* now, you know it will be set in the future. It involves the second coming of the Christ, and the Arimathean is the main character. Beyond that, I'll let you discover it for yourself...

Connie Corcoran Wilson *(www.ConnieCWilson.com) is an award-winning writer, a Featured Contributor to Yahoo!, the David R. Collins Midwest Writing Center Writer of the Year (March 20, 2010) and was the Associated Content Writer of the Year in 2009. She has written more than two dozen books, her latest being "The Color of Evil," (www.TheColorOfEvil.com).*

Other Books By Sean Leary

The Arimathean

(novel)

Does The Shed Skin Know It Was Once A Snake?

(short stories)

Every Number Is Lucky To Someone

(short stories)

Exorcising Ghosts

(graphic novel)

Beautiful Remnants of Chaotic Failures

(poetry)

I Looked Into Her Eyes And Saw The Universe

(poetry)

Danger Maps
(poetry)

Every Broken Heart Creates The Pieces That Will Pave
The Way To The Place Your Heart Will Call Home
(poetry)

Here Comes The Goot!
(children's/beginning readers)

Go, Racecars, Go!
(children's/beginning readers)

Nine Little Ninjas
(children's/beginning readers)

My Life As A Freak Magnet
(humor/memoir)

For more writing and more information, see www.seanleary.com and www.thearimathean.com.